UNFORGETTABLE ROADS

Life is a journey. What is your compass?

Jessica Schaub

Martin Sisters Publishing

Published by

Martin Sisters Publishing, LLC

www. martinsisterspublishing. com

ISBN: 978-1-62553-019-6
Fiction

Printed in the United States of America
Martin Sisters Publishing, LLC

DEDICATION

So many times in the writing of this book, I was side-tracked by life and was compelled to set aside the manuscript to raise a family. My journey of marriage, of motherhood, of writing is certainly not complete, but an endless balance of goals and distractions. God deserves the credit for every word of this book, for He sent me a wonderful husband, beautiful children and a Church I love. Thank you, Abba!

I dedicate this book to all the Alison's in the world who have dreams, to the Jack Elliott's who follow the setting sun, to the Graypay's who cling painfully to the "I should have…" moments. If, on the last page, you find that this story touched your heart, then I dedicate this book to you, for every story should leave a mark and inspire a dream.

June 21ˢᵗ
Alison

The police station was tidy but dust bunnies lurked in corners, shuddering softly as people passed by, affirming only a clean surface. It smelled funny too, like sweat and coffee and stale sugar. Every now and then, a wisp of fruity perfume wandered over, an unintentional gift from the woman sitting near an open window.

It hadn't been a long drive from the hospital to the station, but it was necessary that I do the line-up. Trey stayed at the hospital, so at least Graypay wasn't alone, not that he knew where he was or what had happened. I wasn't even sure I knew the answer to that; we had traveled so far so quickly that it was impossible to remember what state we were in - North Dakota or Montana. Maybe it didn't really matter.

I was here now, in this station, because I had seen his face. It was only for a few seconds, but I remember the depth of his blue eyes, the crease across his forehead, the way his face glared with surprise. He turned and left us there, confused and bleeding.

A police officer sat down opposite me. "We'll do this as quickly as possible, Miss Elliott." He smiled weakly and I knew that 'as quickly as possible' meant 'however long it takes'. "You've seen it on TV; the men will not be able to see you. You just need to tell us if he's there."

I didn't tell him I grew up without a TV.

"There's just a bit of paper work to fill out while we wait," the officer slid a clipboard across his desk.

As I reached for the pen, the officer saw how badly my hands were shaking. "Here," he gently took the pen back. "I'll help you. When is your birthday?"

CHAPTER ONE

Served With Cream and Sugar

May 17ᵗʰ

Alison

I woke to the smell of bacon and eggs, found a new fuzzy robe on the end of my bed, and a card that had been slipped under the door. My seventeenth birthday was off to a good start.

The kitchen sizzled with excitement. As I stepped onto the tile floor, Mom, Dad and Graypay broke into a boisterous chorus of "Happy Birthday". I couldn't pronounce "grandpa" when I was two-years old and 'Graypay' stuck. Even his friends call him Graypay now and it fits: he's all grey.

Mom poured my first cup of coffee, sweetened with milk, vanilla, and sugar. For years, I woke to the smell of coffee. The rich aroma was delicious. Despite all my requests for a sip, I was denied, told that when I was an adult, I would join the ranks of the caffeine addicts. Until then, it was water, milk, or juice.

All the years waiting were not in vain. Although I imagined the taste to be different, richer and less bitter, I drank it all. The warmth of adulthood spread through my arms and legs and I sighed, feeling very pleased with myself.

I know what you're thinking. Seventeen is not the legal age for an adult. Eighteen is. My parents married when they were seventeen. They started their own business after seventeen months of marriage. I was born seventeen months after they moved into this apartment. Yes, I was born on the seventeenth of May. Sadly, there is no seventeenth month of the year – that would round it all off quite nicely. Lucky for me they didn't go so far as to name me Seventeen or some equally horrible name. Alison suits me just fine.

Graypay sat in his usual chair, drinking his coffee from the same mug, wearing the sweater vest he always wore in the morning to 'keep the chill off his heart'. He looked to my dad, eyebrows raised. "Now?"

Dad breathed in, a slow, deep breath. He was stalling. Or preparing for the wind to be knocked out of him. "Now."

Graypay smiled widely and leaned forward. "Alison, do you remember what number 17 on your list is?"

This time I took a deep breath. Was he about to say what I thought he was about to say? "Yes."

"Happy Birthday!" He raised his arms and stood up. "We leave when school's out."

My reaction at this was…well, I'm not proud of it. I've been raised to respond to things calmly. Except Graypay was handing me one of my dreams and it was, without a doubt, the best birthday present I have ever received – or ever will receive. Still, I pride myself on being unlike the other girls, all giggly and silly, but today I was. I jumped up and down, screaming and crying. I hugged Graypay and screamed some more.

Next month I can cross the first thing off my list.

Alison's List of Things to Do and Places to Go:

1. Tour Washington D.C.
2. Put a penny on Abraham Lincoln's knee.
3. Make a wish in Trevi Fountain in Rome, Italy.
4. See Old Faithful.
5. Hike through a mountain pass.
6. Follow the trail of Lewis and Clark.
7. Take my picture in front of a Redwood tree.
8. Be a missionary for at least a year in a third world country.
9. Ride a steamboat down the Mississippi.
10. Visit the pub that C.S. Lewis and J.R.R. Tolkien frequented.
11. Write in my journal at least once a week.
12. Read every book on the banned list.
13. Be an 'extra' in a movie.
14. Go to Christmas Mass at the Vatican.
15. Graduate from college.
16. Have an article published in a magazine.
17. Drive across country. Not on highways, but back roads, and never on a toll road!
18. Work on a cruise ship.
19. Read from the Bible every day.
20. Volunteer at a Soup Kitchen each Thanksgiving.
21. Take the tour through Anne Frank's Secret Annex.
22. See the Great Wall of China.
23. Listen to what my body is telling me; my health is my choice.
24. Drink a mug of beer in a German pub.
25. Buy a bottle of olive oil in Italy.
26. Visit every state in the United States.

27. Learn the provinces of Canada.
28. Speak another language well enough to have a conversation and not be thought a fool.
29. Learn sign language.
30. Write a book.
31. Never eat 'fast food' again.
32. Go camping at least once a year.
33. Sponsor a child in another country.
34. See every Shakespeare play performed on stage.
35. Read the book before seeing the movie – in all cases.
36. If and when I meet a celebrity, I will not act like an idiot.
37. Solve a real mystery.
38. Drive on Highway 1.
39. And Route 66.
40. If I do become a mother, I will do it right, making my children my first priority.
41. Drive Highway 2 from the Upper Peninsula of Michigan to the Pacific Ocean.
42. Buy books in hard cover.
43. Buy Christmas presents for children in foster care.
44. Rescue a dog from the Humane Society and give him or her life filled with love.
45. Always tip 20% at a restaurant.

CHAPTER TWO

A Tough Sell

May 18th
Graypay

The morning after Alison's birthday, I slipped a manila envelope under her door containing a map of the Northern states with our route from Chicago to Montana highlighted, using as many non-highway roads as possible, and a note to Alison: *Three is the magic number.* I knew it wouldn't be long before she came to my room.

"Montana?" she asked, sounding not at all pleased.

"It's a beautiful state," I told her.

"Aren't we going all the way to the Pacific?"

"From Chicago to Montana is pretty far. One thing at a time. Let's make that our first stop and see about going the rest of the way when we get there. If there is anything I've learned in this life, anything planned is bound to change."

She crossed her arms. "What's this magic number?"

"Alison, it took me weeks to convince your parents to let us do this. One of the conditions was that we have someone go with us to help. They have their reasons and I can't argue."

"Help with what? Carrying our luggage?"

"Driving. You have your license, but it's been months since you've driven anywhere. I've driven a handful of times since I came here. It will be good to have someone else drive most of the way. Someone younger than me and older than you."

"You've already thought of someone. Who?"

"I haven't asked him yet. His father told me he comes home today. I'll visit him tomorrow."

"Trey?"

I smiled. "Yes."

Alison stared at me for a moment. "He's been away to college for two years. He was impossible when we were kids. He'll be a bear to travel with, thinking he knows everything."

"Then we'll have to set him straight."

She crossed her arms and shook her head. "He never even writes. There is email, Facebook, texting - if I had that on my phone - and good old letter writing, and he never sent a single word to me."

"Then it will be good to have a few weeks to catch up with him."

"I don't like it."

"It's not up to you to like. It was your parent's request and we will honor it."

She sighed and sat down on the stool near my closet. "Fine."

"Yes, well, thank you for the enthusiasm."

"It's almost impossible to feel enthusiastic about going to Montana with Trey tagging along."

"Maybe someday you'll feel differently."

"About Trey?" Alison wrinkled her nose.

I couldn't help but laugh. "You say that now, but I remember when I first met your grandmother. She was feisty. I didn't know how any man could ever love her."

"What changed?"

I looked at her picture on my dresser. "Everything."

"Do you miss her?" Alison asked.

"Only when I'm awake."

"When you're asleep, you don't feel anything," Alison reasoned.

"Ah, you're forgetting about dreams that reveal your fears and your wishes. It's when I dream that your grandmother joins me again."

Alison didn't look convinced.

"Dreams are powerful things, Alison. God used dreams to give Daniel the tools to become great in Babylon. Joseph gained power by interpreting dreams. I've dreamed about your grandmother often enough to believe that when we are asleep, that's when our doubts are weakest and God can speak to us and allow others to do the same. There's no scientific proof to what I'm saying, of course. I'm just an old man."

"What do you talk about?" Alison asked.

"You. She is very interested in you. She asks about your father. Sometimes we'll go back to a happy moment and look at it together. Sometimes she's silly and I remember crazy dreams about her that don't make sense when I wake up."

Alison took the picture frame of Stephie from the dresser. It was a black and white photo from our wedding day. She held a small bouquet of daisies.

"When did you first dream about her?"

"Just before she died. She was in the hospital. It was early in the morning, when she looked at me and smiled. She was

13

always a beautiful woman, even after the cancer treatments took her hair." That was the truth. Something about her eyes became more alive during her illness than even before. Or maybe it was me, searching her face for a way to keep her with me. I held my hand out for the picture and Alison handed it to me. Gazing at the woman I loved had been reduced to a black and white snapshot of one tiny moment, neatly surrounded by a silver frame and tucked under glass to keep the dust off. I wondered for a moment what photo Alison would keep of me. I put it back on the dresser and continued talking; it was either talk or cry. I didn't want to do either, but that was how it was as a widower. Even after eighteen years.

"We talked about the day we met and some of the places we lived. I asked her if she needed anything. She told me she wanted to wear a pink dress the next day. 'Don't let them make me look like a hussy,' she warned me. I didn't know what she was talking about, but I told her not to worry. I'd take care of her." I pulled out a hanky and wiped my eyes. "But that talk, that last talk was a dream. I woke up and she was gone."

"Just a dream? Why couldn't God have given you one last, real moment?"

"Not *just* a dream," I said, "the best dream. I may have been sleeping, but I know that it was really Stephie talking. There is no doubt in my mind or my heart."

"And that's what faith is," Alison said, knowing what I was going to say next.

I laughed. "You do listen to me."

"Even when I try not to," she stood and headed for the door.

"I'm glad."

"Montana," she looked back from the hallway. "Are you sure?"

"No doubts. It will be perfect. You trust me?"

"Completely."

My heart swelled. "Thank you."

CHAPTER THREE

Thirty Dollars a Day

May 19th

Trey

Graypay came to see me today. I haven't seen him since my high school graduation. It's not that I don't want to visit, but college is busy and I've been able to find a job near school for the last two summers. But not this time. I had to come home.

It was good to see Graypay again. He's aged. I mean, he's always seemed old, but he looked much older today. Tired. Wrinkled. His same smile was still there and his stories were just as funny.

I had the distinct feeling that he had been watching for me, which is ridiculous, because the idea of him seeing me come home from three Chicago city blocks away is impossible. And yet, that's what happened. After he made his request, my father finally understood why Mr. Elliott had called him a month ago.

"Do you have a job for the summer, Trey?"

"No, sir. I only came home yesterday."

17

"Do you have anything specific in mind for the summer?"

"Not really. In this economy, I'll be lucky to land anything."

He smiled when I said that, and I knew I had to say yes to whatever he asked of me.

"Well then, I have a proposal for you to consider. I will be taking Alison on a cross-country trip in June and I would feel much better if you would join us. I would pay you thirty dollars a day and cover all your meals and boarding expenses. In return, you will drive Alison and me to Montana and back."

"Jack, you trust my son with Alison?" My dad asked.

"I do."

My dad persisted. "Alison is a young lady. A very attractive young lady."

"Dad," I interrupted. "Alison is just a kid."

"She's seventeen." Graypay said. "You are nineteen?"

"Twenty."

"Then I will put my trust in you for Alison's safe return. For if anything should happen, well, she is still a minor. You are an adult."

"You make yourself very clear," my dad nodded. "Understood, son?"

"There's nothing to worry about. Alison's like a kid-sister." A know-it-all kind of sister, but I kept that to myself.

"Then you'll take the job?" Graypay asked.

Truth was I would have gone with him for a dollar a day. Money is not something I worry about. As long as I keep to the plans my parents have made for me, they fund everything. When the semester ended and I started for Chicago, mom repeated her rules, as if a lifetime of trying to be invisible to them hadn't driven the message home. I was expected to not interfere with their lifestyle, their vacation plans or their careers. I was to find an internship at the university or work for one of

18

dad's friends. Graypay's offer was the answer to staying away from the folks and earning some pocket change.

CHAPTER FOUR

Awkward!

May 22ⁿᵈ
Trey

Mrs. Elliott invited my parents and me over to finalize the plans for the trip, go over the maps, and talk about all the things I already know how to do. My parents didn't come. Dad had a late meeting and mom was in a good book. Mrs Elliott wasn't surprised when I showed up alone, but she did look disappointed.

Alison was there. When I left for college, Alison was gangly and awkward and still…still…well she didn't look like this. She'd grown taller and … you know, changed. Sisters, related or not, should not be pretty. I became the awkward one, especially when Mrs. Elliott glared at me from the other side of the room. Graypay winked.

Yep. This was going to be an interesting trip.

Graypay

There hasn't been a moment since her birthday that I haven't seen her checking her list of things to pack, preparing her notebooks to fit in her suitcase and checking maps and using that computer to find hotels along the way. She knows we are heading to Montana. She doesn't know why.

Fourteen letters. I sent one letter to every church that had been there all those years ago. Maybe there would be someone there who would remember, who would know where she was now or where she had gone. Nine of the letters have been returned unopened and two had been returned with notes saying that she had never been there.

Instead of focusing on what hasn't happened, I'm trying to focus on what might happen. Think positive. I learned that from her. Was she still like that? Would she look at a rain cloud and anxiously wait for the lightning and dance when it finally ripped across the sky? I do. Now I wait for the other three letters in hopes that I can find her again before it's gone. Such a fool I've been, thinking I have all the time I need to do this. The clock is racing against my mind and I don't know how much time I have. That's the kicker! I'm running on a track I can't see against an invisible opponent and I don't know where the finish line is.

CHAPTER FIVE

Too Much Information,
Not Enough Time

June 11th
Alison

Graypay's bedroom is at the end of the hall between my room and the bathroom. It's actually a former storage closet that my parents expanded by moving my bedroom wall and absorbing the linen closet. Mom spent an afternoon painting the walls bright yellow and decorating the tiny room with second-hand furniture. His twin bed is covered with a quilt my grandmother found at a roadside market years before she went home, which is Graypay's way of saying she died. When Graypay moved in to take care of me, my dad tried to give him my room, but Graypay wouldn't have it. "Little girls need room to grow. Old men need a place to sleep."

A dresser and a bookshelf stand guard on either side of his bed. The top of the dresser is uncluttered, only a silver plated clock which must be wound every night and a few framed pictures. They are all tenderly dusted each week – a tall silver frame of Grannie Stephie on their wedding day, a wooden frame holding my father's second grade picture, and my most recent school picture in a white frame. There is small desk under the window with his stationary and pens in the drawer. He still writes letters to his friends, saying he will single handedly keep the post office in business as emailing and texting take over the world.

When I was younger, I would draw him pictures for his walls; big pictures with the sun and a rainbow and little square houses with triangle roofs and a neat path leading up to the front door, the kinds of pictures with the sky clinging to the top of the page and the green grass along the bottom, and nothingness between. Graypay hung the pictures one at a time over his dresser. The last picture I drew for him is still hanging above the dresser. I think I was eleven when I painted it. With a mixture of ink pens and watercolors, I painted our apartment with my parent's deli open for business on the main floor. Graypay and I are at the apartment window upstairs, waving. Mom and Dad stand in front of the deli, holding sandwiches. The earth and the sky touch in this painting, but not in real life. This is Chicago. The sky is held up by tall buildings and the ground is cement. I like the picture better than what I see outside.

Graypay was packed and ready. His little room was empty, but really the only difference was the bed and the dresser – both bare. A dark yellow square on the wall above his dresser reflects the emptiness of the moment. When I move out of my room, it will be very different. My entire life is catalogued on the walls, in photo boxes, on the shelves and, much to my mother's regret, under the bed.

That's what led to my terrible discovery. Graypay never leaves anything out; it is difficult to believe that he has lived here for seventeen years. He carries a bathroom bag every time, leaving nothing in the medicine cabinet. Today, his prescription was sitting on the bathroom counter. The medicine was unfamiliar as was the doctor's name. Not antibiotics or anti-inflammatory medication.

I said nothing to him, just slipped the bottle into his bathroom bag while he was in the kitchen. I needed answers quickly. I went straight to the computer and Googled the medication. In 1.28 seconds I had 34,785 results, the top 200 were about Alzheimer's Disease. The blood in my veins felt like red Jell-o being sucked through a straw. My mind was just as sluggish as I read the first five or six sites.

Alzheimer's.

Alzheimer's is a degenerative brain disease. It doesn't kill quickly and it has no mercy. It takes away bits and pieces of memory until just a shell of a human remains. One article described the spots on the brain as "tangles". Perfect description. Graypay's memories are starting to snag like fishing line. Right now, I can give Graypay a piece of information, a reminder, and he can unravel his memory to reveal a minuscule detail from fifty years ago, and yet he can't tell me what he had for dinner yesterday.

There is another problem with the 'tangles' and the disease; there is no cure. There are a hundred guesses as to what causes Alzheimer's, but no absolute proof. There are medications that can help slow the disease and mask some of the symptoms, but no miracle pill.

I think I know when Graypay was diagnosed. We all knew that he had a doctor's appointment. I thought it was a 'good heart-rate and cut back on sweets' check-up. When Graypay came home from the doctor's office with a bag of notebooks and pens, he asked for all his meals to be delivered to his room until further notice. He stayed in his room for over a week coming out only to stretch his legs and use the bathroom.

I knew something was amiss. My parents told me to mind my business. "He does this sometimes," my dad said, referring to the unique quirks my grandpa was known for, none of which I have ever witnessed. My first taste was sour. I didn't like him spending that much time alone, but there was nothing I could do about it except wait to learn what he was doing. Perhaps "write a book" was on his life list and he was fulfilling that dream.

I walked with him to the corner store to buy more notebooks. "What are the notebooks for?" I asked.

"Just a little project," he said. "Something I think most people find the need for when they reach my age."

That answer satisfied me, going along with my thoughts on writing a book, a dream many want but so few do.

I didn't believe that now. Was his writing project related to the Alzheimer's? With our trip coming up soon, I needed to know. I've never before felt nervous when knocking on his door. This time, however, my heart pounded so loudly, I couldn't hear him answer my knock. He had to open the door to make me stop knocking.

"It's me. Alison," I said.

"Yes, I know you," he kissed my forehead. "Is it dinner time already?"

I held up the plate my mother had sent up from the deli and asked him what he had done all day in his room.

Graypay took the dinner, set it on his desk, and turned to look at me. I had been scrutinized like this before and I could never look him in the eyes.

"You know."

I nodded.

"I know you have wanted to know what I've been doing." He picked up a notebook from his desk. "I've been writing." He set it back on the desk. I looked at the desk. There were eight spiral notebooks stacked neatly on the left side of the desk, two on the other. One notebook lay open on the desk, Graypay's handwriting filled most of both pages.

I walked over and looked at the cover of the notebook on the top of the tall stack: My Earliest Memories, was printed in Graypay's steady hand.

He stood behind me. "Paper doesn't forget."

For weeks, Graypay had been writing. All day while I was at school, he wrote. He wrote after dinner. He even wrote in the earliest hours of the morning. Now that I knew what he was doing, the mystery of the notebooks wasn't beautiful. It was dark and a little bitter. Like coffee.

"Am I in your notebooks, Graypay?"

"Of course."

"It's hard to imagine remembering so much from so long ago."

Graypay laughed. "Well, it doesn't seem that long ago to me. It's more difficult than I thought it was going to be. What I've come to do is write what I remember as it comes to me. One entry might be about grade school, then next about my railroad years."

"You were a teenager when you worked on the railroad?"

"I finished the eighth grade when I was fourteen. I left a few days later."

I couldn't imagine having been on my own for three years, as Graypay had been when he was seventeen. I'm a year away from graduation. The eighth grade is seen as just a step on a long path. After high school there is still college and graduate school in my future. I've never had a job, aside from the frequent weekends that I worked in the deli, which in my mind doesn't count. Working for your parents is not a real job; it's just the expectation of family chores in a different environment. That and school are the extent of my experiences. Times ARE different. Children are coddled, watched over, surrounded with plastic, and tagged with cell phones.

New experiences were in my future. Not the adventure or exploration kind, unfortunately. From what I had just learned about Alzheimer's, it was more of a test of perseverance.

How long would I have until Graypay would no longer be Graypay? I was glad he was writing the journals. Seemed the best way to keep him. Maybe if Graypay would allow it, I could read his journals. Perhaps then I would know how an old man in a sweater vest and brown loafers could be considered eccentric.

"Do not cast me off in the time of old age; do not forsake me when my strength is spent. O God, do not be far from me; O my God, make haste to help me!"
Psalm 71:9, 12

CHAPTER SIX

Rambling Treasures

June 12th

Alison

Certain classes in school appeal to specific genders. Cooking, deceivingly titled "Household Management" is for the girls, as is "Fashion Design" and the afterschool child care workshop, which is actually day care for the children of the teachers in the district where high school kids (mostly girls) spend one hour a day playing with the children and slowly build up to teaching a three-minute lesson. The boys can find projects geared for them in shop class. That's where Lilly, Lucy, and I decided to make our statement: girls shouldn't be boxed up in the kitchen with the children. We enrolled and were sad when no one even raised an eyebrow at our risky venture. Geared up for our defense against the administration as to why we should be allowed to participate in the shop class, we decided that our confrontation might come on the first day of class. All summer we dreamed aloud of what the reaction would be when we walked into the shop: the stares, open mouths, the protests of girls invading a space designated for only boys.

In the end, the reaction was a huge disappointment. Several senior girls were back for their fourth and final year of woodworking and three others were donning jumpsuits to protect their clothing while they rebuilt an engine. Lilly and Lucy realized that we were a generation or two too late to shock the world with women's liberation issues and dropped the class. I didn't. The tone of the room was enticing; I felt a freedom here like in no other room in the school. The teacher wasn't at the front of the class; he was among us. The projects had nothing to do with history or reading or how well a student could memorize information; it was about a creative eye, an established patience, and the willingness to take risks. I grudgingly accepted the real challenge: working with wood. Projects began with practice in identifying different types of wood through the color, wood grain, and smell; pine and balsam were the easiest for me.

For the first two months, I whittled and carved and watched the older students run the skill saws. We drew pictures of what we wanted to build and worked as a team to construct miniature models. It quickly became my favorite class, even more so than literature. I even returned to the shop after school to work. Mr. Carpenter (No joke. That really is his name) stayed until 5:00 every Wednesday to allow us extra time to perfect our skills, to ask questions, to have more than 50 minutes with a task.

In February, it occurred to me that I had forgotten the entire purpose of joining shop class. No one cared, least of all me, that I was a girl. By the end of the year, my team had built rocking chairs, several wooden toys for the local Santa Claus

Bag program, and we took second place in a construction project. We built a raised flowerbed and a staircase leading from the second floor balcony to a patio at an assisted living complex.

Near the end of the year, Mr. Carpenter announced the final project. We had to design a piece with two different types of wood, moving parts, and carved decorations. I chose to make a chest for Graypay to replace the old cigar box, which was held together with duct tape, for his special mementoes. The moving parts were the lid, hinges, and two drawers along the bottom that slip open and had locks. The lid would be carved with symbols of our faith and finished with a cherry stain.

Sketching out the project took almost as long as it did to build because I wanted it to be perfect. I didn't know what Graypay's cigar box contained, but my dad told me that he had always had that box. Anything that important to him deserved to be kept safe in more than an old cardboard box.

The next challenge after the box was finished was to find a way to give it to him. Graypay's birthday is on November 1st and he insists on not receiving presents on Father's Day. He argued that he is a grandfather now and doesn't want to take the focus off my dad. I argued that he, as a *grand*father, should receive twice the amount of attention. He won, stating that geriatrics, like himself, should be indulged whether the request made any sense or not. All that was left was a random Thursday.

I knew if I wrapped it up like a gift, he would feel uncomfortable. He's big on returning the favor, always prepared with something in return. Instead of making a big deal out of it, I simply set the chest on his bed.

He came home from another trip for more notebooks and ink refills, and saw it there. I watched from the door as he ran his hand over the carvings of four bible stories: the loaves and fishes, the wedding miracle at Cana, Jesus walking on water, and the empty tomb.

"It's beautiful. It deserves to be filled with treasure."

"I thought maybe your cigar box could be replaced with this. But I think your notebooks would fit perfectly."

"No. This is too beautiful for the ramblings of an old man."

"Who says the ramblings of an old man aren't like gold?"

He had no answer for that. In his forever-giving way, he tucked all his notebooks into the box and handed the whole thing to me. "I intended these journals for you. I'm naming you keeper of my memories."

"No, Graypay. I made this box for you."

"Alison, I've never been given anything as beautiful as this chest. It's perfectly suited to hold my journals, which were always meant for you."

I made him pinky swear that when we came home from our trip, this box would stay in his room. He promised.

I wasn't the only one who had been thinking of gifts. I set the chest on my desk and noticed a yellow gift bag on my bed. Inside were five books: Sir Walter Scott's *Ivanhoe*, *The Strange Case of Dr. Jekyll and Mr. Hyde,* one of Robert Louis Stevenson's best works, the forever controversial *Catcher in the Rye* by J.D. Salinger, Mark Twain's American Classic, *The Adventures of Huckleberry Finn* and my all-time favorite, *The Lord of the Rings*.

I had read all these before, not just copies of these stories, but these actual pages. Graypay's room had a tall, narrow shelf with books stacked two deep. Every classic he loved, every author he admired, every book that my teachers never encouraged me to read sat patiently on those shelves, waiting for me. Now Graypay had given me my five favorites: a handful of remembrance.

The note in the bag read:

Alison,

These are for you. I noticed that you have read these more than once. So have I. Bring these on our trip for those miles of flatlands and the dark nights that we must wait for the sun. Treasure these stories as much as I treasure the last seventeen years with you – and what a story that is!

Much love and blessings,

Graypay

On the backside of the note was taped a picture of Graypay and my nine-year-old self standing in front of our time machines.

I laughed out loud.

When I was in the fourth grade, I was bit by the bookworm, which left me feverish and anxious: two symptoms were relieved only by trips to the library, bookstore gift cards, and the quiet hours after dinner on the couch next to Graypay. Mom was forever taking the book out of my hands at dinner time and she took away the lamp next to my bed because I stayed up late every night reading. That was all challenged in the fourth grade. The teacher was a dud. Graypay asked what I did in school each day, and I honestly couldn't think of anything. There had been math drills, penmanship practice, diagramming sentences – nothing truly important.

That's when Graypay rescued my mind from the dulling doldrums of drills by recycling two boxes into works of science fiction. One Saturday morning, Graypay led me to the back room and showed me the time machines. Huge boxes from the new refrigerator and stove my parents had purchased stood painted grey and black and edged with blinking Christmas lights. Toggle switches had been glued to the sides, and old remote controls and painted buttons beckoned the imagination.

"I built one for you and one for me," he smiled.

"What are they?"

"Time machines."

"Do they work?" I asked, a little doubtful.

"Of course they work!" he answered. "I tried them out yesterday. I went to the Caribbean and saw the first encounter the native people had with Christopher Columbus." He visibly shivered. "Not pretty."

I still wasn't sure what the catch was, but it was too fun to be cynical. "How does it work?"

"Go inside. I'll work the controls. You can go wherever you want."

"Are there controls inside, too?"

"Yes."

"How do they work?"

"You're a smart girl. You'll figure it out."

"Where are you going?"

He looked up, thinking. "I think I might go to Israel two-thousand years ago." He kissed me on the forehead. "Be careful and I'll see you soon."

"Be careful of what?" I mean, *really*. It was just a cardboard box.

"Some people come back from time travel… changed." He shook his head, and almost looked sad.

"Changed how?"

"Some lose something. Others gain something. A few have been eaten and never return." His eyes twinkled. "So be careful."

"Okay." I opened the door and saw only a chair. Before the cardboard door closed behind me, I caught a quick glimpse of a curtain.

"Graypay?" I stood still. "I can't see."

"Did you see the chair?"

34

"Yes."

"Then sit down," he said. "I need to program the machine. Don't forget to buckle up." Feeling for the chair, I cautiously sat down and felt for the seat belt. I found it, and even in the darkness I recognized the feel of my mother's sequined belt from her high school days. I had used it many times before when playing dress-up. It seemed Graypay also found a good use for it. I fastened the belt through the loop; I had fastened the belt so many times before, I could do it in the dark without a problem. Maybe that's why Graypay chose it.

"Ready?" he asked, pretending to shout through the walls of the time machine as if they were metal.

"Yes!" I yelled back the same way.

"Now, hold on!" The time machine shook; a little at first, but grew quickly into a gut wrenching, I'm-glad-there's-a-seatbelt ride.

"Graypay!" I shouted, a little nervous.

He didn't answer. I was on my way to…sometime.

The machine settled to a hum: a fan just outside the time machine drowned out the noise of the city. A strand of Christmas lights taped to the interior of the box turned on, and the curtain in front of me magically slid open, revealing a lamp and books.

Books. Of course!

Robin Hood. King Arthur and the Knights of the Round Table. To Kill a Mockingbird. Anne Frank. Tom Sawyer. The Hobbit. Ok, so the Hobbit isn't a true story, but it takes place in a time of imagination that exists within each person.

Beneath the shelf that held the lamp and books were all my provisions: pillow and blanket, tissues, a thermos of alphabet soup, and a jug of water. The books Graypay chose were not on the shelves in my classroom. They were not on the shelves in the school library where fourth graders were allowed. They were forbidden, difficult, and wonderful. That first day I chose *Anne Frank: The Diary of a Young Girl*. Seemed appropriate.

And I was right. It was difficult to read, both in content and style. I didn't understand everything, but I understood the cruelty of human nature and the raw love of a family. I saw the little annex where they lived and felt the pain of not going outside. I heard Margot cough as silently as possible so they would not be discovered. Their lack of food made me hungry. My alphabet soup seemed a luxury.

I don't know how long I stayed in the time machine. I always remember Anne's journal at this point when Graypay 'brought me back'. Stopping at that particular point was a gift from God: we all know that we dream most of the night, but many dreams we forget before we wake up. It's when we wake up during a dream that we remember it. The last line I read was: "I shall not shrink from the truth any longer, because the longer it is put off, the more difficult it will be for them when they do hear it."

Just as I finished that sentence, the humming outside my time machine grew louder and the machine began to shake. I quickly climbed back into my seat and fastened the bespangled safety belt. Graypay worked up a sweat bringing me home. When the shaking stopped, I waited for a sign to know it was safe to exit.

"Alison?" Graypay shouted through the cardboard wall. "Alison, did you make it?"

"Yes!"

He opened the door and I climbed out. I looked at him, his eyes fresh and shining, his clothing crumpled from sitting.

"Where did you go?" I asked.

"I walked with Jesus," his hand went to his heart, the way it always did when he talked about Jesus. "And you?"

"I hid from the Führer in a tiny annex."

"You must be hungry," he said.

"Yes!" I answered as my stomach rumbled. "I'll eat anything except beans and stale bread."

I was hungry again as I stood in my room debating whether to read Graypay's journals, Mark Twain or go raid the cupboard. The choice was simple: celery and peanut butter, a glass of milk and Graypay's first journal about his westward escape. It was the perfect Thursday afternoon.

A Small Ohio Town

1946
Jack Elliott

The world was shrinking before my eyes. The shelves at the library were filled with adventure stories of pirates, Vikings, and pilgrims finding new lands. Our country tells wild folktales of giants cutting down trees, and accounts of wagon trains headed into the Wild West with Prairie Schooners sailing over the grassy waves, cutting a path to a new beginning. I was afraid those kinds of adventures were extinct. In the 1940's when most people had a car and a telephone, and the land was cut with roads and strung with electrical wire, what was left to explore? Folks believed that everything that could be invented had been. The United States was explored and mapped. All my life, I dreamed of traveling and exploring new places, of making discoveries and befriending folks who knew the land. I wanted to walk the trails of Lewis and Clark and see the West before it was parceled and sold and built up into one metropolis after the next. I needed to get out there, to see it.

I found a way. The answer had been under my feet, I just needed to recognize it for what it was. On the way home from school, I was thinking about Lewis and Clark and how they studied the plants and animals and managed the entire trip to the Pacific with the Corps of Discovery, when I tripped on the railroad track. There it was: a direct line to the West. All I needed to do was hop on a train and go. I didn't think it would be the adventure that Meriwether Lewis had, but I was desperate to bend the Core of Discovery rules just to get away.

For weeks, I planned my escape, hording my coins from my after school job, until Pa found my handkerchief filled with money and asked me what I was saving up for. I knew a beating would follow; it always did after he took the time to talk to me. Now that he knew I had been saving up to leave, it was inevitable. He asked and I told him the truth.

He didn't start in with his fists, so I kept talking, hoping that he would grow bored with my idea, forget about the money and go off for another drink.

I was wrong.

The next day at school, I told my teacher that I had fallen off the ledge in the barn. She bought it. I didn't have any lunch that day, a punishment from Ma for keeping good money from her, which was just as well. My lip was so swollen I don't think I could have eaten anything.

I went to work after school and tried to hide my face under my hat. As I was about to leave for home, Mr. Howard saw me. "Your pa's handiwork on your face is getting more noticeable."

"Oh, no, Mr. Howard. I fell off the ledge in the barn."

"Jack," Mr. Howard lit his pipe, "I know the mark of a fist. Your pa should be in jail for what he done to ya'."

I didn't know what to say. All the times before, people had accepted my lies. Mr. Howard, however, saw right through them.

"Please don't say nothing. I don't want my pa to be in trouble."

"Hmph." he puffed on his pipe. "You want to go out into the world then you need to learn to speak well. It's, 'Please don't say anything'. What did you do to deserve this... punishment?"

I told him that Pa found my money for the trip and took it all. The bruises were a reminder to not keep money from him again. A postcard of the Rocky Mountains, a card I had bought months ago from Mr. Howard was always in my pocket as a compass to my dreams. I handed it to Mr. Howard and described the herds of elk and the few buffalo that were left. The library had books about the west and that out there, where stars look like God's glitter, cast across the black dome of night. There were Indians too, living on reservation and trying to hold onto their way of life while the world of whiteness covered every bit of their past, blinding us all.

Mr. Howard listened to my stories of how the West wasn't really won at all if you think about what was lost, and how I wanted to be out there, how I dreamed of seeing the mountains and walk the trails of the first explorers who only explored and didn't destroy.

He didn't laugh at me. He puffed on his pipe and looked into my eyes and saw a boy's dreams. He never laughed at dreams, for they are the slight string that pulls us from one day to the next toward a star that has our own name on it. My star was out west. My star was wild.

"That's a good plan, son," he said. "How much you figure you need to get out there?"

"Train ticket plus twenty dollars ought to do," I said. "I intend on working my way out there on the railroad."

He nodded, thinking. "You'll keep your extra money with me. I've a safe place in the house."

"But, Mr. Howard, there won't be nothing left to save if I give it all to my pa."

"I'm going to give you a raise. It will be a secret just between you and me. I've no love for your pa for how he treats you. Jack, you are a fine young man. Fact that you are kin to that drunk is a surprise to all who know you both. I'd like to see you get away from there as soon as possible. I figure that anything I do to help that happen would be a good thing. You need a place to stay?"

"I don't think Pa would appreciate me not coming home. Not that I'm ungrateful," I added. "Just don't want to leave Ma there alone. If he takes his anger out on me, he leaves Ma alone."

"I see." Mr. Howard didn't like that, but he respected my plan. "You'll finish school first. An adventure is no good for a fool."

"Yes, sir."

He reached into his pocket and gave me a dollar. "Keep your grades up and there will be another one. I see a great future for you if you exercise patience and wisdom. Do you know how you can find wisdom? She's an allusive lover to many."

Wisdom? Allusive lover? I was certain they didn't teach about that in school. I said no.

"Proverbs. The beginning of wisdom is: get it; at the cost of all you have, get understanding."

I nodded my head and said, "Yes, sir", but I really had no inkling of what he was talking about. What I did know was that I didn't like the sound of it: "at the cost of all you have." How are wisdom and understanding different? And what was I willing to pay? What was I willing to give up getting wisdom?

I wonder, had known what it would cost me, if I would have ever left home.

CHAPTER SEVEN

Of Funerals and Inappropriate Dancing

June 13th

Alison

Have you ever read a poem? I'm not talking about Dr. Suess or Shel Silverstein with silly stanzas about selling baby brothers, but poems in which every word packs a punch. Poetry that lingers in your mind, not because of the rhyme, but because of the words and passions it evokes. My English Literature teacher taught my class how to wade past the words and swim into the meaning, diving past the lack of rhyme and enjoying the strokes of rhythm. Good poetry beats in the heart, the careful syllables illustrating emotions.

My favorite poet is Emily Dickenson. Her work is utterly depressing at times, but I don't read it to be cheered. It's a look into fears and thoughts I have about my own mortality. It's an honest look into what happens between the heart and the mind.

The Bustle in a House
The Morning after Death
Is solemnest of industries
Enacted upon Earth —
The Sweeping up the Heart
And putting Love away
We shall not want to use again
Until Eternity.
                                   - Emily Dickenson

I've only known one person who died, Eleanor Connor, a friend of Graypay's. The morning after she went home, my parents, Graypay, and I took sandwiches to the house to feed all the family members who were staying with Henry, Eleanor's husband, and helping with the funeral preparations. The house was oddly quiet with only the frequent sniff and hushed voices on the phone with the funeral home. There was so much to do and not much time to do it and no one wanted to do anything. Henry sat at the kitchen counter and held his cup of tea. He didn't look like he'd been crying so I felt comfortable talking to him.

"I'm sorry about Eleanor," I said as I sat down next to him.

He turned and patted me on the cheek, "Thank you, Alison. Would you like some tea?"

"No, thank you."

He took a sip of his tea and studied my face. "You don't want to be here, do you?"

I looked down. "I don't mind."

"I don't want to be here either," Henry whispered to me. I looked up and saw his face. I didn't understand the expression; there was sadness in the way his eyes seemed too heavy to keep open, but there was something about his mouth that gave me pause. Was he smiling? Who could smile the day after someone they love died? How long do you wait to feel happy again? Certainly not one day.

"I turned on Eleanor's music, but my daughter turned it off. I know what dress Eleanor wanted to wear, but my daughter thinks she'll look better in the black dress."

"Isn't black a good color for a funeral?" I asked, agreeing with his daughter.

"Maybe for some people," Henry sighed, "but Eleanor and I talked about this day. Whoever was the first to meet our Heavenly Father, the other one was to celebrate the life, not mourn the loss."

Graypay joined us. "Marylyn doesn't want to follow Eleanor's plans?"

"Thinks they're ridiculous," Henry said.

"She's hurting," Graypay said.

Henry nodded. "We all are. But there *is* something to celebrate. There can be joy this day."

"Well then," Graypay said as he walked away, toward my mother, a plan brewing in his head. He whispered in her ear. My mother shook her head and blushed. After a few exchanges, she sighed and nodded. Graypay kissed her forehead and nearly jogged out of the room.

Marylyn followed him, her eyes angry. I knew she had heard Graypay's plan and I realized what he was after. I slipped away from Henry and followed them.

"Absolutely not!" Marylyn said to Graypay. "It's undignified."

"It's what they planned," Graypay said.

"No one does this. It's not normal," Marylyn said, her voice tight with tears.

Graypay rested his hand on her arm. "And that's what makes it so special. Your parents loved each other. Honor them by letting Henry have this last moment."

Marylyn's face streamed with tears. "It's ridiculous. People will talk."

Graypay smiled. "They sure will. You can pout like a child or you can make your father happy."

The funeral was the next afternoon. Tension and sadness rode visibly on Marylyn and Henry's faces. The only person who looked peaceful was Eleanor.

It was very strange to be at her funeral, to see her lying in a white casket lined with sky blue material and silver handles. The viewing, where the deceased is lying in a coffin for all to see, stirred conflicting emotions. On one hand, I wanted to see her again. On the other hand, she didn't look like herself. Death changes people: those who die are made up to look to be only sleeping and those still alive walk around like death is sitting on their shoulders.

Eleanor was old and wrinkled, but I never saw it until that moment. It was the life within her that made her shine. Eighty-two years old. I never knew her age because she never acted her age. Henry and Eleanor danced together every night while listening to an old-style radio, the big wooden radio that takes up space on the floor, has dials and a light behind the numbers. Graypay and I joined them many times, spinning and twirling like tops. I was the only fourth grader who knew the Fox Trot and the Waltz.

After buckets of tears had been cried, the funeral directors closed the casket and six men, nephews, a neighbor and my dad carried her across the street to the church. I don't know what the priest said, I just know that we all sat there, stood during the Gospel reading and sat again, then followed Eleanor out the door. We drove in relative silence to the cemetery where the priest spoke again about returning to the earth.

That's what I remember most clearly – returning to the earth. It seemed oddly comforting. I like the idea that when it's all said and done, my skin and bones will become earth and my soul will belong to God. The priest talked about eternity in heaven with God. That's beyond my understanding – eternity. Forever. If I were to empty out the Pacific Ocean cup by cup, the time that would take still wouldn't be forever. What will we do in heaven? Do we have tasks? Missions? Chores? Will I know that I'm dead? Will I like heaven? Is it the pain of death the thing that people fear? Or, is it that no one understands the concept of eternity?

I stood there between Graypay and my mother and tried to imagine the happiest place I knew. Nothing compared to the idea of heaven. Eternal light. Eternal grace and joy. What on Earth could compare to that? A really good book? A cup of hot cocoa on a cold winter day? The sun shining through the yellow and red maple leaves in October? All those things come to an end - the last page, the last drop, the last leaf. The promise is that heaven has no end. I like that.

Those thoughts distracted me through the cemetery service and the ride back to the church hall for the luncheon. After crying our eyes out, we were amazingly famished. I didn't think anyone would want to eat, but there was very little food left after we had all gone back for seconds.

The priest, at Henry's request, had set-up a microphone in the church hall. As people took their plates to the kitchen, Graypay walked to the microphone and Marylyn walked out of the room.

"Good afternoon," Graypay's voice boomed through the room. "My name is Jack Elliott. Henry and Eleanor have been

47

my dear friends for longer than I'm willing to admit. I'm sure you all know that the two of them danced their way through marriage, through parenthood, through the empty nest years. The dance of life, it is often called, is a beautiful thing, a gift from God. Henry and Eleanor knew that. Their dance was one that took them through all the good times as well as all the rough times." Graypay nodded to me and I hit 'play' on the CD player.

My mother took Henry's hand and led him to the center of the room. Henry smiled at my mother and said something softly to her, which made my mother giggle through her tears. The music filled the room and Henry danced. I'd never seen my mother dance before, but she was good. She allowed Henry to lead her and together they were lovely.

Henry found his joy in the music. He danced with my mother like the whole world depended on the rhythm of his feet. For me, I cried not because of Eleanor's death or Henry's loss, but because life stood up and announced itself to me that day. I saw the love of a family come together through a death. I saw my mother dance for the first time. I saw Marylyn wince as people watched with smiling faces and tear-filled vision. As Henry spun my mother around the room, he closed his eyes and let sorrow leak from his eyes.

I think Emily Dickenson was wrong.

The Bustle in a Heart
The Mourning after Death
Is Healthiest of Industries
Enacted to Music
The Sweeping of the feet
And dancing for Love
We shall have to see again
Upon Eternity.   *-Alison Elliott*

48

Before our trip, Graypay and I went to visit Henry 'for one last cup of tea,' Graypay said, which sounded very permanent to me. Graypay and Henry reminisced about their days as Park Rangers and all the people and places they remembered from their traveling days. I think the fact that Henry and Eleanor had settled in Chicago to raise their family was a big reason why Graypay agreed to stay with me for so long. Having other restless souls nearby eased the tension of being in one place for so long.

Henry had one request from me: one last dance with him before we left.

"We've danced dozens of times," I said. "I hope we will dance again."

"Today you are a girl," Henry said. "I believe when you come home, you will be a woman. Give me one last dance before you are all grown up."

1946
Jack Elliott

It's not often that we understand the moment when we are in it. Your first day of high school is important, just like the first time you drive a car without your parents, or when you graduate. Those days have "take my picture" written all over them. Those are the moments that hang on the walls and showcase great days. Those are just mile markers for life; moments that we check off as we pass by. They are important, but everyone can have them.

It's the big moments that spring out at us like monsters in a funhouse that truly shape who we are. There are no pictures of these days. The only documentation of these big moments are the bruises on our spirit and the toughened skin as the lessons of life make us stronger.

It was Mr. and Mrs. Howard, not my parents, who introduced God's love to me and taught me what is right and what is wrong. It's wrong to worship other gods, like money, fame and things that can fall and break. It's wrong to kill. I must obey my mother and father even though they beat me. I'm not to worry about what I don't have and focus on the gifts from God I do have. Don't swear, steal, or lie. It's simple and straight forward and almost impossible.

I left home a year and a half after I tripped on the train tracks. I earned all A's in school and Mr. Howard stayed true to his word and gave me money for that hard work. I chopped wood, rode Mr. Howard's bike to run errands for the pharmacy, picked apples, trimmed trees and even swept the halls of the school for extra money.

When I left home after eighth grade graduation, I felt like a rich man. I had fifty-five dollars in my pocket and a train ticket to the West. Mrs. Howard packed cheese sandwiches and gingerbread for my trip. I told Ma I was leaving and she gave me a burlap bag of apples. With that bag and another bag of clothing, I boarded the train to the West, to discover what was out there beckoning people toward the setting sun.

I told Pa good-bye. I told him that I was leaving so I could be a man; not a man like him who drank and fought with anyone he felt like, but a man like Mr. Howard. Pa was angry and he came after me, intending to tie me up in the barn until I got this idea of leaving out of my head. Mr. Howard knew of my plans and thought it be best that I not be alone when I told Pa about my train ticket and brought the sheriff out. I was very thankful for that.

When I left home, Pa was in jail, and Mr. and Mrs. Howard stood on the platform of the train station and waved. I don't know where Ma was.

I had dreamt about that first night away from home for months. I would be free from everything that made me a boy. There was no turning back.

That night was the first night away from home. The first. Not the last. Ahead of me lay the whole world. When the darkness outside made the window a mirror, I found the dining car and ordered a cup of coffee. It kept me awake all night, so I didn't miss a moment of my first night of freedom. I was on my way.

Half-way through the night, I reached into the bag from the Howard's and found a wrapped package. It was a bible. Mrs. Howard, in her flowing calligraphy had written:

Jack,

I'm proud of you, son. You had a dream and you are making it a reality. No man can do everything alone. You've heard the priest talk about God's compassion for us. Never forget that. No matter what you encounter in your life, remember that God is never far away – even when it seems that mountains are separating you from Him. This bible is for you, to keep you in God's Word so you can continue to grow into a man that God will bless abundantly.

We love you like our own,

Mr. and Mrs. Howard

"Do nothing out of selfishness or out of vainglory; rather, humbly regard others as more important than yourselves…" Philippians 2:3

Good ol' Mrs. Howard. She had fed me with food and now had provided a way to feed me every day in between.

CHAPTER EIGHT

Great Expectations

June 14th

Trey

I half expected the car to be a cardboard box. In all the afternoons and weekends I spent with Graypay and Alison, we had made a castle (Alison's idea, not mine), a rocket (my idea!), a puppet theater and cardboard puppets all out of boxes from the deli. While I knew the car wouldn't be a former refrigerator box fueled by my shoes, I expected an economy car, something that was affordable, something easily lost in a parking lot.

That was not what Graypay had planned.

He must have stashed every penny away for the last seventeen years. The car he bought for this trip was a 1957 Chevy, two-door, V8 Turbo Fire engine, baby blue with white stripes down the side, white leather interior and gigantic fins on the back. An auto icon. The front was round and smooth, the chrome polished to a gleam. Inside, the steering ball on the wheel was a polished oak sphere and the radio had dials and a red bar that slid up and down the numbers. When I turned on the radio, I heard static! Actual static! There was no tape or CD player and no dock for my ipod, so that bit. Who would care in a ride like this?

They don't make cars like that anymore. I could sleep comfortably in the trunk. Even after we packed it, there was room for more. Graypay packed the most: his bag, a wooden locker – the old-fashioned kind with metal clasps, a carved box, and a bag of books. The look in his eye when he said good-bye to his son was not what I expected. There was a permanence to it; a finality that I wasn't expecting. Perhaps it was the long hug he gave his son, or the extra kiss to the forehead of Alison's mother, but he wasn't saying, "See you when I return."

I'm not certain, but I don't think Graypay intended to return to Chicago, and Alison was the only one who doesn't realize it.

Seeing Stars

Alison

I had bigger ideas than this. A train car for starters, not a car, no matter how antique it was. Just me and Graypay, not Trey. I thought that at some point Chicago would end. The highway pointed the way to the west, but the buildings continued for miles and miles, hours and hours.

I don't know what I expected. Ok, that's a stupid thing to say. I knew exactly what I expected. I Googled this route and switched the view from 'map' to 'satellite' view to see the distance from Chicago to Montana section by section.

It was far. It took almost thirty minutes to view the entire trip. Now that I was here, riding in a car, seeing every inch of the road, it was a huge disappointment.

Part of me, the romantic part I suppose, the part of me raised on a constant diet of Graypay's stories and the obviously larger-than-life dream of what a real journey is, hoped that the satellite pictures were misleading, that there were open spaces filled with the wonders of nature and picturesque historical markers placed far from the road noise and kept free of litter by devoted followers of the old ways. What greeted me instead was pavement, conveniently painted with reflective strips and edged with rumble strips, barbed wire and hideous billboards announcing the next deep-fry pit.

Trey drove, Graypay stared out the window, and I manned the map, the cooler and the backseat. The miles took a full

55

minute to tick off. I wondered if all the things on my life list would begin with this same anti-climatic aura.

"This is like a needle," I said to Graypay when we stopped for a snack and bathroom break about six hours after leaving Chicago.

"What do you mean?"

"My dreams of launching into my first road trip were an image of waving good-bye to mom and dad and seeing new things. If that was a bubble, then today was a needle. This highway, the litter, the utter lack of open spaces. That's nothing new. My cross-country trip was supposed to show me new things and wasn't supposed to include Trey, of all people." I glanced over to where Trey stood, leaning against the car while the gas chugged into the tank.

He looked happy.

Graypay told me to make the car my new 'bubble'.

I tried to reclaim that adventure by finding something pure and untouched by man. At a roadside motel, after Graypay was in bed and Trey was trying to make himself comfortable on a cot, I stepped outside to look at the stars. I've seen the computer-generated visions of our night sky at the planetarium, but I've never seen all of Orion or any of the constellations in Chicago. Too many lights and buildings in the way. Surely, a full days' drive away from the big city would reveal the true night sky. Our hotel was on the outskirts of Duluth. I saw Orion and the Big Dipper. Found Polaris and Draco. That was more than at home, but I wasn't satisfied. The Milky Way was hiding behind a shield of city lights.

Trey came outside to check on me. "Are we following the North Star on this trip?"

"Thankfully, no," I said. "With all this light pollution, we would be lost."

"We don't have a GPS. We could still lose our way."

"A little confidence for the navigator, please." I tried to sound nice, but really, he was just as annoying as always.

"So far so good," Trey looked around at the sky. "We didn't get lost today." Out of the corner of my eye, I saw Trey turn his gaze from the stars to me. "You look disappointed."

"I thought there would be more stars."

"There are. Not here, though. I mean they're here, but hidden."

My neck was growing stiff. I looked into the dark horizon. "Have you ever seen the Milky Way? I mean, outside of the planetarium? Have you seen it in the night sky?"

"In Hawaii."

"Do you think we'll see it in Montana?"

"I hope so. The stars, when I saw them in Hawaii made me feel so...important."

I didn't want to encourage him to keep me company, but I couldn't imagine what he meant. "Explain," I said.

"Most people say that the stars make them feel small. Insignificant. When we were on vacation, I had the nights to myself because my parents left for business meetings. Our hotel room was on the sixth or seventh floor and a balcony overlooked the beach. Mom paid the concierge to make sure I stayed in the room and out of trouble."

"You never tried to sneak out?" I asked.

"She paid him *very* well," Trey said. "So the only place I felt like I wasn't imprisoned was on the balcony. The stars were there too.

"The concierge felt bad for me and the from the second night until the day we left, he brought me books about stars and constellations. Then he borrowed a telescope from a friend and let me use it the last two nights.

"I stayed up almost all night star-gazing, hoping I would discover a new star. I thought maybe if I did something amazing," he stopped and cleared his throat, "I still like looking at stars. They never change." He glanced at me quickly and looked away. "I sound stupid."

"You always sound stupid," I teased, "but I think I understand."

Trey raised his eyebrow at me, wordlessly challenging me to explain.

"This is my first time outside of Chicago. Sometimes, Graypay and I would go to the roof and try to see the stars. It was so frustrating, not being able to see what I knew was out there."

Trey looked down. "The stars were always there, even when no one else was."

I didn't know what to say to that. I had always known that Trey's parents were very different from my own, but until this moment, I didn't realize how deep that difference drove a wedge in Trey's heart. All their money, their fancy apartment, their exotic vacations were charms that dangled in front of me, taunting me with a life I didn't have. In Hawaii, Trey's only companions were the stars. That made me sad. Then I felt a gut-punch of guilt. If I were left alone like that in Hawaii, would the stars have made me feel important or insignificant?

Dear Diary... Bah!

Trey

Let me just make this very, very clear. This is not my idea of a summer vacation. Sure, Graypay is a great guy and all, but he won't allow the TV to be turned on and now he's making me write in a journal. Graypay and Alison are both scratching away like mad, writing down every little thing that happened today.

Well, I can sum that excitement up in two words: I drove.

We left Chicago early this morning and drove. We stopped for three meals, and I drove in between. At the last rest area, I left the keys on the counter in the men's room. I knew that as soon as I set them down it was a bad idea, that I would likely forget them and have to come back in. I wasn't worried. It's not like I could drive off without them. They are the only keys to the car.

But Graypay worked himself into a frenzy and had me find a store to buy a notebook. So here I sit, writing about my day like some dear-diary-girl.

Dear Diary, I'm in Hell. The TV is two feet away and I'm not allowed to turn in on.

I've known this for years, but it's always such a shock when it comes up again: Alison grew up without a TV. She never watched Scooby-Doo or a reality TV show. She never came home from school, grabbed a snack and watched the Cartoon Network. I can't imagine what she did every day without a TV! No silly commercials, no one-liners from programs to repeat with friends, no anger toward the DVR when the record program feature bumped off a show I hadn't watched yet. She has no experience of watching the clock to catch her favorite show, or racing to the bathroom during a commercial and trying to get back to the couch before the show starts again. "To be continued...," that week-long wait for the rest of the story, means nothing to her.

Graypay does have a radio, the old-timer type that stands about three-and-a-half-feet tall and looks like a piece of furniture. I remember it from when I was a kid. When my parents were working late, I stayed with Graypay and Alison. We listened to National Public Radio for the news, then Family Life Radio. Those evenings were filled with Paul Harvey and Adventures in Odyssey. The stories on the radio were always fun, the kind of fun that camping is, the doing-without kind of joy. I also knew that I could go home later and watch a show. That never happened for Alison. I wonder if she knows what she missed. Was she was ever angry with Graypay for getting rid of the television? That was his doing. When he moved in with Alison and her parents, he did so under a few conditions, one of them being 'No TV.' Does Alison know that was one of the conditions? It doesn't change how I feel about Graypay. He's the type of man that everyone likes – even when you don't.

One time Alison and I argued over a toy. I don't remember the specifics, but I do remember that I hit Alison. Not proud of it, but, hey, I was a kid. Graypay was mad, *really* mad, I could tell even though he didn't yell. He came over to me and kneeled, scooped up Alison and made sure she wasn't hurt too bad.

"What did you do?" he asked me, his voice was steady, his eyes sharp.

"She wouldn't give me the toy!" I tried to explain.

"I asked you what you did. Not why."

"But that's my toy," I said.

"What did you *do*?"

I didn't know what to say. He knew what I did, but I didn't want to say it. Surely, the gravity of the situation, Alison not giving me what I wanted, was enough of a reason to explain my actions. I stood there, waiting for Graypay to drop the whole thing, and he kneeled there, eye-to-eye with my eight-year-old frame, waiting for me to fess up. I don't know how long we stared each other down, but the game was growing old.

"I hit her." I whispered it so I could claim that I told him but he just didn't hear me.

"Louder."

"I hit her."

"And did hitting her get you what you wanted?" Graypay asked. "Are you having fun now?"

"No."

He nodded. "And what will you do the next time someone won't do what you want them to do?"

I had no answer. It was my understanding that if you wanted something, you did everything you could to get it. I shrugged my shoulders. I think Graypay knew me better than I knew myself. He offered up a few suggestions: compromise, taking turns, bringing an extra toy. I remember liking him even more after that. He never yelled, he never blamed me for hitting because he knew I wasn't born pre-programmed knowing all the rules. He simply worked with me to think of better options for next time.

Would I have learned that lesson had a TV been turned on? If I hadn't gone home that day without his words going through my mind, would I have fought again at school the next day?

Who says that the TV makes the nation? It's a tool to share information, but it is abused to 'get the ratings'. Do I really want to fall under that bus? How different will my life be if I don't watch television ever again? Or, what if I only pick one show a week to watch? Which one would I chose? Oh, this is going to be hard. I know that I can't go back to my weekend movie marathons without feeling that incredible guilt.

And look at me! I wrote more than two words.

Eggs in Baskets and Old Men with Fires

1948

Jack Elliott

I wish I had kept a journal during my westward adventure, but I was too young to see the value in that. I thought I would always remember every new thing, all the faces, the places, the feelings. Everything was new and exciting and wonderful and I thought it would last forever.

Maybe that was my first lesson: nothing lasts forever. If someone had told me, "You know, son, try to appreciate what you have while you have it," I would have scoffed and walked away. My youth had lasted thus far…the western wilds were still thriving in spots…America was a strong country…how could any of that change?

I was rich. I was free. I was a man.

I was also stupid.

Mrs. Miller always warned me to never put all my eggs in one basket. I thought she meant it literally. She raised chickens and collected the eggs in baskets and we kept them in two or three locations throughout the store, just in case. I should have divided my money and carried it in two or three different places: my wallet, my shoes, and my bag. Perhaps it would have been better if I had glued it to my chest.

As I sat on that train watching vast landscapes and dinky towns pass by, I imagined my life as an adventurer – hopping on trains, seeing the world, meeting interesting people until there was no more land. Then, after this place, when this beautiful land became tired of my feet, I'd take a ship and venture off American soil into the treacherous depths of the ocean. My imagination planned treks through the Chinese countryside, a stroll along the Great Wall, an expedition into India, then Africa and Europe. The Atlantic would be my final hurdle. After touring New York City, I'd head home via the Great Lakes, filled with wisdom, aged by the winds of the world and ready for whatever my heart desired.

Some of those dreams still haunt me, calling for one more try to be the man I thought I would be: a man with global ideals and a treasure chest of stories.

As it was, I started my global expedition on a train to the state of Washington to find work.

The train stopped for a few hours in North Dakota; time enough to unload and load the train cars with merchandise and passengers. I'd seen a sliver of the country from the train window as we chugged on by. It was time to meet the people, see the landscapes, and search out a hot meal.

I did all those things. I met an old man with a tire, the sheriff, and Six-String Sam.

By now I was familiar with the schedule and the way of train stations and felt confident enough to leave the train yard and walk around town a bit to see if all the towns this side of the Mississippi were constructed of cardboard and tin. It may sound like a strange reason to explore, but after hundreds of miles and dozens of towns, the majority of the buildings appeared as sturdy as card houses.

I left my bag with the starched man behind the ticket counter. He gave me a small claim ticket and tied a matching ticket to my bag. With a small nod, he pointed to a sign nailed to the wall:

No Claim Ticket – No Luggage

I tucked the ticket deep into my wallet and left the clapboard station to find sunshine.

The streets were arranged at right angles and lined with comfortable houses with nice lawns with tall grass. Along the main street, I found a General Store with a candy counter and a soda fountain. I splurged for a Cherry Coca-Cola and a sandwich. I wandered the aisles for a bit, but I didn't need anything – just the few clothes in my bag and the money in my pocket. Life was full of possibilities and I was a prince, far from classrooms, parents, and expectations.

About forty-five minutes before the train was scheduled to leave, I strolled toward the station. I had ventured away, but I certainly didn't want to miss the train and be left behind. Around the corner of the gas station, an old man wrestled a tire into his trunk. I jogged across the street and offered to help.

"Right fine of ya', young man," he said.

"Mister, I don't think this will fit with all these bags…" I recognized my bag in his trunk. "Hey!" A blasting pain on the back of my head exploded, knocking every thought and all my senses out.

When I came to, the old man was gone with my wallet and my bag, but he left that old tire behind.

CHAPTER NINE

Mirages

June 15th
Alison

I have heard roads described many different ways: ribbons, cuts, dividers, paths to civilization, destroyers of nature, makers of men, scars… The list goes on.

There are definitely different kinds of roads, different levels of beauty, and style. The most picturesque is the country road cutting through a tunnel of tree branches. It doesn't matter if the trees are heavy with spring blossoms, aging with the color of full summer or sleeping under the cover of ice and snow – the road is beautiful and belongs on a postcard.

Then there are dusty roads littered with trash and people. Smog, rats, trash bins, pee – all the sludge of humanity seems to collect in the gutters and flood the streets when God sends his rain to try cleanse His wayward children. It's hard to feel clean when you are knee deep in a gutter bath.

And there are the 'in-between roads'. The streets crowded-in with retailers and restaurants. There are streets with traffic lights telling us what to do and when. There are sidewalks sometimes, but fewer pedestrians as we distance ourselves from the city. These streets are not beautiful and not even practical. They are simply streets to get from point A to point B and sell everything you could need or want along the way. Why can't city and building designers spend a little extra time to beautify the space between A and B? Why can't a retail section look as stunning as the historic neighborhood? And why don't more people care?

I admit it. I expected to drive and see something amazing in every mile. I thought the food would be better. Rest stops and gas stations and underarm odor were never in my daydreams about traveling across the country. Boredom robs the miles between stops.

The first day out of Chicago was too dream-like for me to have been fully objective about what I was seeing. Besides, the first half of the day I saw things I had seen before. (I may not have been able to claim ever leaving the environs of Chicago, but I had been to the suburbs.)

I blamed all the books that I'd read; I believed the United States to be more beautiful, with smiling people and cleaner roads.

Therefore, in the spirit of Emily Dickenson, I composed a poem:
Green Grass
City Captive
barbed streets and cement mazes
trap me.
Escape to Green
Fields of Hope for amber waves
free me.
The Greener grass
Planted just out of my reach

haunt me.
Heaven on earth;
  happiness found movies
  deceive me.
White-washed wheels a
  key to city cells and a
  greener me.
Costly freedom,
  the price too great to fully
  please me.
Hum of rubber
  the gentle song of pavement
  lulls me.
The Greater Plan
  despite my view, is not all
  about me.

- Alison Elliott

Alison

"Have you put any thought into where you want to go to college?" Trey asked during one of our stops.

"Anywhere outside of Illinois."

"That desperate to get away?" Trey laughed.

"It's not that. I like Chicago, but everyone should have an opportunity to stand on their own. I need to be far away from my parents so I can do that."

"What if you fail?"

"I can't fail," I looked at him. "Even if I were to skip classes and not pass tests, I wouldn't call that failure."

"Most people would," Trey said.

"Most people aren't thinkers."

Trey rolled his eyes. "Okay. I'll bite. What do you mean?"

"A marathon. If I trained for months to run a marathon, and the day of the race I didn't win, is that failing? I finished the race. That's success."

"What about the people who don't finish the race? Or the people who train, but decide not to run?" Trey's face was pinched, the deep crease on his forehead aging him.

"Then they learned that they are not runners. Maybe if they look at what they do enjoy, they will find a different race, a different calling. That's not failing."

"My father would say it was," Trey pushed the dirt around his shoes.

"You're in medical school. Is that what you really want to do?"

"I don't know." He threw his hands in the air. "There's so much pressure to do well, to go to medical school, to have a big career and a big paycheck so I can have the respect of others."

It was challenging to wait for Trey to continue. I was bursting with ideas, suggestions, and advice. I bit the inside of my cheek. Now was not the time to talk. Now was the time to listen.

"I don't want to disappoint my parents," he continued. "I've spent so much time worrying about their plans for me, I've made none of my own."

"What are you going to do?" I asked.

"What can I do?"

"First, start dreaming." I stood. "Dreamers think of wild possibilities. Graypay always says that."

And that got me thinking. There is more going on here than I'm realizing. One…a trip. Two…a present. There is always a third thing. What is it? Will I like it? What am I missing? Dreaming of wild possibilities, I can imagine a million different outcomes to this trip. Will it be everything I expected?

As Graypay would say, "Patience answers all questions."

71

1948
Jack Elliott

Rage.

That's what I felt.

Pure rage.

Storming down the street with my brain pounding from the conk on the head courtesy of that old man with the tire, I exploded through the train station door. Images of beating that train station attendant to a pulp fueled my charge into a battle that I hoped would bring justice and satisfaction. Being robbed was never a part of my dreams of my westward travels.

Penniless.

I had nothing. How was I going to eat? I didn't work for two years, giving half my money to Pa so he could go get drunk, so that some other old fool could do the same.

Every ounce of fury I had built up every time Pa's fist met my face now sizzled between my skin and muscles. I was dynamite with a short fuse; unstable TNT. Just let anyone step in front of me and a spark of anger would light and I knew I would explode like a fire cracker. I didn't even care if I hurt anyone. Revenge was all I wanted.

The train attendant turned quickly as I pushed the doors open, banging them loudly into the walls. "You!" I shouted. Several people looked at me with alarm. *Good!* I thought. *Let them see how this train station is run.* "Someone stole my bags!"

"Certainly not," the train station man said. He was not the same man who had given me my claim ticket. "No one can get back here except employees."

"I left my bags here. A man loaded them into the back of his car."

"What man?" he asked.

"I don't know. He had my bag. He took my wallet and all my money."

The man glanced at the luggage cubbies. "Maybe it's still here. Hand over the ticket and I'll check."

"He took my wallet!" I shouted. "My claim ticket was in my wallet!"

Pointing to the sign, NO CLAIM TICKET, NO LUGGAGE, he shrugged. "Without the ticket, I can't give you your bag."

"My bag isn't here!"

"Then why are you looking for it here?"

That was it. This idiot didn't understand that I had been robbed; didn't see that his co-worker was a shady cheater. Or maybe... "You're in on this together! You and that other fellow sell people's luggage to that old thief."

The tension in the station grew perceptibly thick. People came up behind me, demanding to know if it was true, wanting to see if their luggage was still safe behind the counter.

"The boy doesn't even have a claim ticket," the man shouted, defending himself. "You see the sign. He probably is just trying to stir up trouble, looking for a free meal or a free ride."

I snapped. Launching over the counter, diving into the forbidden zone of "employees only" I did everything within my power to pound that man's face into the back of his skull. Fortunately for me, I never had the chance.

From among the gathered people, three men grabbed me from behind the counter and pulled me out of the station. A full-blown riot had started, and I still didn't have the satisfaction of hitting someone.

"Let me go!" I struggled against their strong arms. Cigarette smoke burned my nose as one man hushed me.

"We're helping, boy!"

"I don't want your help!"

"Come on," the man holding my hands said to the others as they dragged me further away from the train station. I was being kidnapped. Some westward adventure. First I was robbed and knocked out. Now I was being abducted. If I survived this, I would have one heck of a story to tell.

"Stop kickin', son," the man warned again. "We ain't planning you any harm."

So far they hadn't, but we were still within ear shot of the train station. If they were smart kidnappers, they would wait until we were far from everyone. I settled and they set me down.

"Hit a batch of bad luck, son?" the oldest of the three men asked. His voice surprised me. Or the tone of his voice did; he wasn't forceful like a kidnapper should be. He seemed...concerned.

I nodded. "I was robbed. I have nothing left."

A younger man scoffed. "You're still alive. Hopefully you still have your wits 'bout ya after that display."

"He robbed me! They cheated me!"

"Likely true," the older man said. "But nothing doin' 'bout it now."

"Then what do I do? That old man who robbed me even took my train ticket. I'm stuck here." My adventure was not going to end like this.

"One thing at a time," the younger man said. "Look for work."

"But what about tonight?" I asked. "Where am I supposed to sleep? How can I pay for a bed without any money?"

The third man chuckled. "There's always a way. Hell, half this country was built on the backs of men with less than you."

I had no idea what he was talking about. The look on my face must have made that obvious.

The older man nodded. "Six-String is right. Stick with us and we'll get you started."

"Six-string?" I asked. "What kind of a name is that?"

Six-string pulled a tattered guitar from behind his back. "I'm the music man. Six-string Sam."

"I'm Ice Box Bill," the older man introduced himself, "and that's Coupling Paul."

I took in their appearance: clothes worn thin and patched as best as possible, and a large bags slung across their backs. Army-issued canteens draped their shoulders and a small flask stuck out of Ice Box Bill's back pocket. "You're hobos."

"That's right," Ice Box Bill smiled. "We're on our way to Washington for the apple-picking season."

"How?"

Ice Box Bill motioned with his head toward the train. "That side-door car is empty. Just as the train is 'bout to leave, we'll catch out."

"Is that legal?"

They all shrugged.

"Times makin' it necessary," Ice Box said. "As long as we don't hurt the cargo or the train cars and keep to ourselves, most engineers and brakemen don't mind."

"Unless you run into the Nazi," Coupling Paul added.

"A real Nazi?" I was suddenly very nervous.

"Could'a been, far as I'm concerned. He's the yard man a few towns west of here. He don't see a difference between hobos, tramps or bums."

I honestly didn't either. "Aren't they all the same thing?"

Coupling Paul pointed a finger at me, "I ain't never gunna be taken for some bum. Tramps? They's less to worry about, but I know a few who give even them a bad name. No, boy. We're hobos. We are travelin' the rails lookin' for work. Honest folk."

I was glad to hear that.

The train whistle sounded and a flurry of passengers boarded the train.

"Listen, son," Ice Box Bill said, "we've gotta catch out. Why don't you come with us? You was supposed to be ridin' this train anyways. What difference would it make if you were just a few cars back? Still gunna get where you was headed."

Very true, I thought. My adventure was well under way: robbed, kidnapped, and now a hobo. Had great potential.

CHAPTER 10

Long Forgotten

June 16th
Trey

I'm writing this after a very long, very confusing day. We are somewhere in South Dakota. I don't even know the name of the town because Alison has the map but hasn't said a word since it happened. We stopped here for lunch. Alison thought it would be a good idea to stretch our legs and walk around town for an hour or so. Graypay said he'd been here in his youth and that he would enjoy walking around to see what's changed and what's stayed the same. I jumped at the chance to find some time alone for a while. It's not that driving is hard – stay between the lines and follow Alison's directions – but it's the constant company, the droning conversation followed by lingering silences that wears me out.

After lunch, we each went our separate way with the agreement that we would meet at the car in one hour. I don't know where Alison and Graypay went, but I escaped before they could pull me into some reminiscent tour of the town.

I was at the car a few minutes late, but I was the first one there. I waited for another ten minutes before the anger set in.

Finally, about twenty minutes after we were supposed to meet, Alison came running down the sidewalk looking for Graypay.

"Have you seen him?" Alison asked me before she stopped. "I can't find him."

"Relax," I said and leaned back against the car. "He doesn't walk as fast as he used to. He'll be here."

"No, we went that way together," she pointed down the street. "He wanted to show me the church. We went inside. He left and I thought he was looking for the men's room, but he never came back."

I'll admit, that made me nervous. Graypay is all about knowing where we are. It wasn't like him to just wander off and not meet us. Alison and I stood at the car looking up and down the main street. Graypay didn't have a cell phone on him. This was a small town, but big enough to lose someone.

"Get in," I said to Alison. "Let's go to the church and look there first."

Alison

Going back to the church was a good idea. I knew he wouldn't be there, but it was a good place to start. At least, that's what I kept telling myself. It just didn't make sense! Why would Graypay wander off like this? Ok. I knew why. I've heard on the news about people with Alzheimer's wandering away from their homes and getting lost. That's *other* people. Not Graypay.

"Is this part of your grandfather's plan?" Trey asked.

"To scare me by disappearing? To leave me alone?" I asked.

"You're not alone," Trey said.

"No."

Trey glanced from the road to me. "No?"

"No, he's not doing this on purpose. That's not his style."

"So what is this?"

I didn't want to answer. I knew what it was. Did Trey? Did he recognize the fever with which Graypay was pouring his mind onto paper? With each day that passed, another indicator walked in and announced the imminent arrival of the end.

A few blocks away from the church, I saw Graypay. He was racing down the road, his face red with the effort and twisted in pain. Trey screeched to a halt and parked alongside the road.

"Graypay!" I yelled, but he didn't hear me. "Graypay!" Trey and I ran up to him.

"You!" he said to Trey. "Have you seen a little girl? She's so little and she wandered off. Have you seen her?"

79

Trey looked at me, confused. My stomach plummeted. I read about this in my research. Sometimes Alzheimer patients will become confused and relive a moment that may have happened thirty or forty years before; usually a traumatic event.

I stepped forward and touched his arm. "Graypay, it's me. Alison." He looked around and shook his head. "No, she's missing. She was right there and then she was gone."

"There's no one here, Graypay," I told him. "We don't live here."

"Did you used live here, Jack?" Trey asked. Jack. Trey never called Graypay by his first name.

"No. Not here." He focused his eyes on me. "Ah. You're not lost."

"I'm here."

"Good. Good. Let's go, huh?" He shuffled back to the car, seeming so much older than he had only an hour before.

Come Back to Me
Oh I think I shall never see
A thing so tragic as senility.
It steals your life, a history
of treasures hidden mentally.
From the depths of reality
It comes, leaving a family
without a sound patriarchy
What is it? Only cruelty.
Where once was strength – fragility.
A lifetime of tales now stands empty.
I have but one final plea –
Let my Grapay come back to me.
-Alison Elliott

Regrets

Trey

It was a quiet ride after that town. Not peaceful. Just silent. Graypay slept in the backseat, exhausted by whatever had happened. Alison was as lost in her own thoughts as I was. This episode gave me a name for what was going on.

Alzheimer's Disease.

Graypay has it. There is no doubt. All the little mysteries around this trip came together. He was giving Alison the best thing he could – himself. The man he was just a year ago was evaporating like water under the sun. This trip was their moment to finalize whatever was between them. Perhaps a time for Alison to understand him better.

I was here to be a safety line for the both of them. I agreed to come because I needed the work. I quickly learned it would be grueling. I didn't know it be like this. Emotions are not my thing. It's better to keep moving forward and accepting whatever changes come along. After all, life is constantly spinning out ahead of us. It just seems that it's just easier to take it as it comes than try to hold on to something that is out of our reach. Graypay is falling out of Alison's reach.

We drove until the sun was resting on the tree tops, blinding me. I found a little roadside motel with decent prices near a restaurant and gas station. I filled the tank, and brought a meal back to the hotel room so we could go to bed early and leave again tomorrow morning. It seemed a good idea at the time. Looking back, however, I should have kept driving.

Alison

There was no safety ring to toss in front of him while he struggled against waves of confusion. Alzheimer's. An ugly word. Say it. It tastes bad. Hear it; it sounds wrong. See it. It hurts the heart, makes lungs tighten, and fills the stomach with sour lead.

I watched as Graypay struggled up the sidewalk, calling and searching for her.

Her.

Not me.

Her.

In the seconds that ticked by, as I touched my grandfather's arm, in the moments that he searched my face and didn't see me, in that interminable instant, I felt authentic terror.

What surprised me most was the dread of what stood in front of me: an Alzheimer's demon possessing my grandfather. What alarmed me most was the cruel truth that I wasn't 'her' and had no idea who 'her' could be.

When you love someone, there is little you wouldn't do for them. In that place, that glimmer of time, I would have given anything to know who Graypay was looking for and find her and bring her to Graypay so that he might be himself. Another part of me shriveled and cried when it was clear that I wasn't enough for him. Me, Alison, was not the one for whom he searched.

Who is 'She?' That question lingers between my shoulders, tightening every muscle, making my head ache. We found a hotel, had dinner and tucked Graypay into bed. He joked about being so old that we were treating him like an infant. It wasn't funny to me.

After Graypay fell asleep, I slipped outside and sat at a picnic table, pouring over his journals by the light of a flashlight.

Trey joined me a short while later.

"Find anything interesting in Jack's journals?" he asked.

I didn't answer for two reasons. One, Trey had never called Graypay Jack until now. It was like he was trying to be more grown-up. Second, I *had* found something. I handed Trey the notebook that had turned my stomach. Trey, being Trey, read it aloud.

August 1954

I always hoped that someday I would fall in love. I hoped she would be pretty and sweet and that when she would see me coming home from work, her whole face would smile. Mostly I wish for that because when Pa would come home, never from work but from wherever he had been drinking, Ma would suddenly rush into a cleaning frenzy to finish the last little bit of her chores so that Pa wouldn't have any reason to hit her. I will never hit a woman. Pa never saw how much Ma worked around the house, doing the laundry, growing the garden, making meals. She never had much to work with, but none of us starved. So I've spent my youth and now my independent years praying for someone to love. I just never thought it would be so wonderful.

She saw me walking toward Ruth and Jacob's barn after working all day in town. She slipped away from Ruth and came to the barn, giving me a huge hug and a big kiss. Yes, dear Lord, I love this little lady. I pray that I will honor her and always do what is right, for never should a sweet thing like her suffer a moment longer.

"He really loved your grandmother," he handed the notebook back to me.

"This isn't about my Granny Stephie. They met in 1960."

"I didn't know Graypay was married before your grandmother."

"He wasn't."

"Then who is this?" Trey asked.

"I don't know. Graypay has never talked about her before."

"Well..." Trey looked grim.

"Yeah." I closed the journal and put it back in the chest, where I hoped the secret of this other woman would remain, buried like a curse.

"Isn't this what you wanted? To see the world? To discover the adventure your grandfather had when he was young?"

"I thought so. The stories in the books are always interesting and safe. In all the years I've listened to him talk about the West, I never pictured this." I looked at Trey. He wasn't laughing at me, so I felt safe to tell him more. "And books never reveal things about your grandfather, things that go against everything he has ever taught me."

"Your grandfather is a good man."

"Now he is. The more I read from his journals, the more—" I stopped, not because I didn't know what to say, but because the tears had started, and I didn't trust myself to not sound ridiculous.

"The more human he becomes." Trey finished the sentence. Silence lingered like static cling for several minutes, giving my mind more than enough time to imagine several possibilities: Graypay was using this trip to find this woman. Maybe he was looking for the child they had together. I know that is a huge leap, thinking Graypay could have another child, but my mind was wrenched open to all possibilities, especially after today's incident.

"Can I be honest with you, Alison?"

"Aren't you always?" I sniffed and wiped my nose on the back of my hand. Darn tears.

"Well, yeah. I'll ask permission this time. I suppose this is more along the lines of honest advice. May I?" He continued when I nodded. "I've always admired your grandfather. He is kind and his faith astounds me. I like the idea that when he was my age, he wasn't like that. It gives me hope that I can still learn to be like him. That I will someday have enough experience under my belt to know what to say and how to say it."

"You think that having an affair is admirable?"

Trey took the notebook out of the chest. "This doesn't read like an affair. Your grandfather wasn't married to your grandmother and this person. . . well, there is nothing here to suggest that it was anything but a mutual love. We don't know anything about her: where they met, how long they were together. Maybe they just dated." He started to open the journal again, but I put my hand on the cover to keep it closed, hiding Graypay's handwriting inside and hoping that it would also keep the threat of discovering this truth hidden too.

"What happens if the mystery reveals something I can't bear?"

"You won't know that until you figure it out," Trey answered. "Maybe it will help you when you learn who she was. Maybe you are supposed to learn that people are people. We all make mistakes, but we aren't defined by them."

I turned to Trey. "I can't figure you out."

"What do you mean?"

"One minute you are the biggest jerk and the next you're showing compassion. Which is it?"

"Why can't it be both?" Trey asked.

"You know what Graypay would say to that, don't you?" I teased.

"It would be a verse from scripture, wouldn't it?"

"Yep."

Trey sighed, "Which verse?"

"The book of James. Chapter three I think. I don't remember the exact wording, but it basically says that our mouths are like springs and a spring can't bring forth both sweet and brackish waters."

Trey laughed. "And, of course, we are only supposed to gush good things."

"Isn't that what you want to do? To say things that build people up?"

"What if it's not true?" Trey challenged.

"I'm not suggesting that you lie, but if you look for the good in something, you'll find it. Look for the bad; you'll find that too."

"And you always look for the good." Trey shook his head sadly at my obvious ignorance. "Don't you see how that makes you weak? If you aren't prepared to handle a difficult situation, then you'll be trampled."

I sighed. "I'm not weak. At least I don't feel weak. I prefer to see the good. It makes life nicer. I see the bad too, sometimes I can't miss it, but I don't think that makes me weak. I think that makes it easier to like people, to get past their short-comings and welcome who they are where ever they are."

"Do you like me?" Trey asked.

"No. Not very much." I meant it, but I laughed as I answered him.

Trey frowned. "I suppose you don't. I'm just too honest."

"Yup. That must be it. Honesty. What a horrible characteristic."

Trey sat quietly for a long time. I didn't leave. I knew Trey well enough to know that he was brewing a question and that I needed to be patient. "So looking for the good…you always find it?"

"Always."

"But your life has been so easy." Trey said. "I'm mean, nothing really bad has happened to you."

There was no arguing with him. My life had been extraordinarily easy. My parents were still alive and married, I had been raised by a loving grandfather while my parents worked, but early in the morning and at night, we were all together. There had been no sicknesses, no tragedies, no economic trauma. So, yes, it would be easy to see the good when surrounded by all good. "You're right. My life has been easy. I hope that the joy I know will stay with me when something does go wrong."

"Hmm." Trey sighed.

"You disagree?" I asked.

"I do. If you are accustomed to warm weather, you could never truly understand the sharp sting of an arctic winter."

"Or," I challenged, "The memories of the warmth would sustain me."

"Just like your grandfather." He nudged me gently with his shoulder.

1948
Jack

Traveling in box cars is far from comfortable, but the advantages were in the company. Six-string Sam played his guitar as well as anyone I heard on Mr. Miller's radio. Stories as sweet as syrup poured from these men. Ice Box Bill had been a Sergeant in the Army during the war, fighting in Northern Africa mostly, although he had also been to Germany and Italy. Six-String Sam and Coupling Paul were veterans too. It would have been perfect if Six-String and Coupling were soldiers under Ice Box's command, seeing how Ice Box was obviously the leader of this trio, but they had met on the tracks a few months before.

"What's your name, son?" Ice Box asked.

"Jack Ell—"

Ice Box held up his hand. "Naw, not your given name. Your rail name."

"What's the difference?" I asked.

"Rail name's earned."

"Like Ice Box? What's that mean, anyway?"

The old sergeant laughed. "Well, I caught my first ride out of Chicago, where the yards have hired men to keep folks like us from ridin'. I needed to catch out quick, so I hopped into a car I knew they wouldn't check." He shivered at the memory.

"Ice Box," I thought for a moment. "A refrigerated car?"

Six-String's shoulder shook with silent laughter as he continued the story. "That's how Ice Box and I met. I was in Minnesota ready to dodge a yardman when I saw Ice Box come tumblin' out. Nearly dead and blue, he was."

"Sam and I were quick friends," Ice Box said. "He offered me his canteen."

"Water?" I asked.

Six-String handed me his canteen. "And I offer it to you, Bare-back Jack."

With my rail name earned, I gratefully took Six-String's canteen and felt the burn of whiskey all way to my bare back. Coughing and nearly losing the few contents of my stomach, I handed that blasted canteen to Six-String while the three men laughed.

As Bare-back Jack, I had to rely on these men for everything. Realizing my dread at being a burden, they assured me that once we reached Washington, I could find work and once again be on my own. "Until then," Coupling Paul said in his quietly gruff voice, "you'll be one of us."

And so I was...for a whole week.

Traveling on a train without a ticket, riding in the open-door cars, seeing the country for free, was an experience. I met some incredible men that week. Overhaul Paul was the largest man I had ever met. He was quiet and quick to laugh, wore overalls that had been patched so much, I assumed that his name came from this. Henry-the-Track was tough as nails with a quick temper and a quicker fist, but he fought on my side when a not-so-nice drifter tried to steal my coat. Pole was a lean, lanky fellow with a rich Polish accent and a winning hand at poker. Just in the one night we stayed over in the jungle, he won almost fifteen dollars.

I didn't know what a jungle was, and I was so tired of not knowing anything, that I kept my mouth shut and just figured that at some point I'd learn. We left the train somewhere in the middle of Montana. We hadn't actually traveled that far west in the week I'd been riding with them. Six-string hopped us all on a train that went south when we heard rumor of work in Colorado, but by the time we got there, we only had work for one day. We rode north toward Montana again with intentions to head to Washington. Near the Rocky Mountains, we didn't get on the next train, but headed for the jungle, which was a Hobo Camp. I was eager to meet other hobo's and hear their stories. Boy, I wasn't disappointed. The jungle was a mile or two from town, near the river. Two trees served as the roof, and it was far more than we needed. We bathed in the river and washed our clothes. Many of the men carefully tended to repairing rips in pants and coats. I was only at the jungle for one night, but it was one of the greatest nights of my life.

In all my dreams of coming out west, of discovering the beauty of the land, I had never once considered the people. What a fool! Something about the country, the mountains in the distance, the freedom from walls and roof, the constant search for food and water, opens a man's mind to what's truly around him. What we wore didn't matter as long as we wore something. Where we came from was far less important than where we were going. The most important thing we carried, wore and shared were our words. The tone with which we spoke, the stories spread over meals, the smiles and handshakes, were like money exchanged.

With our plan to go to Washington for apple season, we had two obstacles before us: one, the Rocky Mountains; two, the Nazi.

The Nazi wasn't German or even in the Nazi party. He was a yard man in Williston, North Dakota. From the tales I heard in the jungle, getting past the Nazi was like hiding from the Gestapo.

We rode into Williston late at night, jumping off the car in complete darkness and following Coupling Paul as he lead us into the safety of the nearby woods. We spent the night under the cover of clouds and rose early to catch out for Washington State.

Catching out is sometimes a quick jump into a car as the train begins its acceleration out of the yard. One other time, we had to dodge the yard man twice before we found an empty car.

As the sun rose, we saw the train yard from our hiding place. "There he is," said Ice Box, pointing to a short man wearing overalls and a striped conductor's hat. In his hand was a clipboard which he wrote on then tucked the pencil behind his ear. On his belt was a holster with a pistol near as long as his thigh.

"Can he really shoot that thing?" I asked. "Looks about to knock him over if it went off."

Ice Box laughed bitterly, "Don't let his size fool ya. Likely the last thing you'll ever misjudge."

As we scouted the yard, we watched the Nazi check the cars, and watched which cars he had already checked so we could jump in those. Just as Nazi would walk around a car, he seemed to reappear thirty feet away. "How's he do that?" Six-String whispered even though the Nazi was more than fifty feet away.

Ice Box sighed. "No idea. He's quick."

"Why the gun?" I asked.

"Takes his job seriously," Six-String answered. "If we get separated, let's meet in the next town. We'll wait for anyone left behind for two days. That should give us time to catch up after the stay."

I didn't like how he said 'the stay'. "What stay?"

"The rumor is that the Nazi has a jail cell just for hobos."

"Jail?" I swallowed. Jail time was certainly not on my list. "How long?"

"Usually just for the over night. Course, there have been a few who have never been heard from again."

"You mean he—?" I pulled my finger across my throat.

Coupling snorted a laugh. "You've some 'magination, kid."

"No one knows for sure what the Nazi does to hobos, unless you would like to find out for yourself," said Ice Box. "But I don't believe that he would use that gun on a human being."

"Then why carry it?" I wondered.

"Men who carry like that are afraid. He's not big but that gun probably makes him feel ten-feet tall."

Ice Box patted my shoulder, "Time." He dashed out of the coverage of shrubs and ran towards the train. I was the last one to reach the train, and was having a hard time keeping up with the accelerating cars. "Come on, kid!" Coupling shouted. "Pick up your feet!" He reached further out and Six-String held onto his other arm. "Reach!"

I reached and picked up my feet, but something tangled between my feet and I tumbled head-over-heels down a small bank of stones. I heard Coupling shout, "Two days!"

"Yeah. Thanks," I muttered, feeling bruises pop up all over my back and arms. Then I felt something else press into my back.

"You're welcome."

I turned to see the Nazi, standing behind me with his foot-long pistol aimed right at my heart. From where I was sitting, he did look ten feet tall.

"Yer far young for a hobo," the Nazi said in a surprisingly nasal voice.

I thought it best to not say anything.

"Come on," he waved his gun indicating that I should stand up. "I've got a place for you to stay today."

"Jail?" I asked.

"That's right. Folks who steal deserve a few nights behind them bars. Does a man good to accept his punishment."

While that last bit was something I agreed with, I wasn't about to go to jail. Hoping that Ice Box was right about the Nazi not actually using that gun on people, I turned tail and ran. With no bags or guns weighing me down, and perhaps because jail time was chasing me, I outran that yardman easy. Grass, trees and insects flew by as I ran away from the tracks, that farthest I had been from that steel spine since home.

Slowly, my legs started to cramp if felt a sharp pain in my side. I fell to the earth, and rolled to my back, looking at the sky. As the cramp eased and my heart stopped beating between my ears, I realized that although I had outrun one problem, there were several more awaiting me: I was alone, broke, and now lost.

Taking a lesson from Six-String, I searched my situation for a gem. That's what he said to do when nothing seems to be going the right way. It took me the better part of the day, but I finally decided that walking has advantages. Whereas on the train the countryside chugged by as I lazily watched, walking allowed me to feel every stone on my path and completely memorize the landscape before it slowly metamorphosed into another.

At home, I read the books about Lewis and Clark and how they found food. It didn't help me much. I found a few overly ripe berries and a stream of water. By nightfall I was a miserable, hungry, sore-footed mess. Just after the sun finally dipped below the horizon, I could see a few lights far off. A town? Farm? It didn't matter. I had no money to rent a room, so when my feet refused to take another step I lay down in the long grass and looked at the sky.

The shock of being robbed, separated from Ice Box, Coupling and Six-String and now on the run was stoking an anger which kept me warm during the cool evening. The display in the sky calmed me. It didn't happen right away. It was a gradual revealing, a deliberate transition from darkness to luminaries of light. I lay on my back and looking up, I only saw shades of blue and purple and stars. Not just the Big Dipper and the North Star, but clusters and clouds of stars. I knew how to find Orion and Draco and Cassiopeia, but I had always star-gazed from my own backyard. When I was bored with craning my neck, I only had to go inside to bed. Not this night. I had no bed. I had no backyard. In Montana, the sky knows no end.

My crazy imagination was stoked hotter than a five-foot camp fire, and I thought of all the stories those stars knew, picturing them all up there staring down at this earth and knowing that no matter what great feats man could accomplish, nothing would even compare to the blazing power of a star.

Thoughts buzzed in and out of my head, droning me into a stupor. All evening I had stewed over my situation. I had been too full of pride. I had viewed this western adventure as a success only if I had money. Yet here I was, dirt poor, sleeping in the dirt, witnessing the heavens. If I had not been robbed, not met the hobos, I'd have missed this. The more I thought about what I would have missed, the more comfortable the earth felt, the more the stars shone.

In all the glittery glory of the night sky, I wondered why some people feel small in the world. Folks back home would fret over problems. "God don't care about me." "Why would I be important to the world?" The answer was in the stars. I don't know if I can explain it – it was a revelation, a feeling I have never doubted: I was right where I was supposed to be. All the stars appeared to be caught in a dark dome around the earth. I always thought the stars were scattered like seeds across the heavens. That night I understood that God hadn't just tossed the stars around. He had placed each one just so.

The world lost its pull on me that night. I saw no ground, no trees, no mountains, only the never-ending sky. If I dulled my senses just a tad, I imagined floating high above the ground, just like a star. A vast eternity had been spread out before me, a demonstration of possibilities and countless beauty. I noticed that the clouds of stars were brilliant, but fuzzy. It was the stars that stood alone that shone more vibrantly.

I was one star that night, placed just so in that field somewhere in Montana. Maybe God scattered my life's belongings away so I would shine brighter. Maybe, like the constellations, I needed to be here. There was a reason. I knew deep in my heart that I was not alone, nor forgotten.

Afraid?

Yes!

Worried?

Some.

Alone?

Never.

All that may sound a little preachy, but I learned it that night. I didn't believe the Miller's or the priest at church when they told me about God's love. I had to go way out west and lose everything I owned in order to really find God.

Time went unnoticed in the dark. The moon slyly roamed among the stars, whispering night noises. I don't remember closing my eyes, but I woke quickly when a foot nudged by arm.

"You dead?" a voice asked.

"Dead folks wouldn't answer," I said, sad to realize my evening with the stars had ended.

An old man stood over me, his face obscured by the rising sun behind him. "Figure so," he chuckled.

I stood, wet from the dew and suddenly chilled to the bone.

"You lost?" he asked.

"Not really."

The man raised an eyebrow.

"It's a long story."

"I'll take the short version."

"I was headed out west, was robbed, traveled with hobos, and yesterday I was chased out of the train yard."

He dusted his felt hat with his hand, thinking. "Sounds like quite an adventure."

"Yes, sir." I couldn't agree more.

"You planning to keep heading west?" he asked.

"Can't," I shivered and wrapped my arms around my body. "Broke."

"You have plans to do something 'bout that?"

"Well," I really didn't. "Look for work, I suppose."

CHAPTER 11

Major Setback

June 17th
Alison

It's a small thing – forgetting to shave. I wish he could have just smiled and said, "Oh, this? I'm growing a beard." Even if it was a lie, that would be better.

Instead, he expressed utter confusion.

Graypay may have been standing right there, but he was as lost to me as yesterday. One of the signs of Alzheimer's is forgetting to do daily things. Shaving. Graypay has never had a beard or a mustache. He shaves every morning before breakfast. When I asked him about it, he reached his hand up to his face to feel the stubble.

Trey tried to help alleviate some of the tension, "Jack, if you don't want to shave, we can head out to breakfast."

Jack.

Trey called him Jack again.

And that seemed to snap him out of it.

"Oh, no. I'll…um…take a few more minutes to do that. If you don't mind?"

"No problem," Trey nodded and hauled his bag out to the car.

I carried my bag out to the car and found Trey searching the trunk with way too much fervor. "Lose your wallet?" I teased. He was constantly setting things down and leaving without them. First the keys, then his bathroom case at the rest stop.

"Did you take his chest into the room?" his voice was muffled with his head nearly under the back seat.

"No. Why?"

He crawled out of the car, his hair rumpled. "I brought the chest out to the trunk last night after we read, but it isn't here. Look at this." He leaned close to the key hole on the trunk. "There's a scratch here and the key hole is bent."

"So what?" I said, completely unimpressed by his forensic investigation.

"I think someone stole Graypay's journal chest."

"Why? Who would steal a case of notebooks? They are only valuable to me!" my voice was escalating out of control.

"Alison, I don't know. Let's check the room again. Maybe Graypay took it in there."

But he hadn't. If my reaction to the news that the chest had been stolen was fiery, then Graypay's was nuclear. Beads of nervous sweat dripped from his brow as he tore apart the room and the car, searching for something that I knew was no longer there. "My journals…my journals…" he muttered again and again as Trey went to find the hotel manager, an overly tanned grandmother named Bee O'Bee wearing a tube top and silver flip flops.

"Don't you have video surveillance?" I asked.

"Nope."

"Let's call the police," Graypay said. "We need to get those journals back."

Bee snapped her gum, "Not likely to come out all this way."

"Why?" Trey asked.

"Funding cuts. Only left is Garth. He's a retired Sheriff's Deputy whose five shades to the west, if you know what I mean."

I didn't, but I took it to mean that Garth wasn't going to be helpful at all.

Bee gave us directions to the police station and wished us well. Trey gave her his cell phone number and a request to call us if she found something. She didn't look excited to be given a task beyond passing out room keys and collecting money, so all my hopes rested on a semi-retired man named Garth.

Graypay was frantic on the way to the police station. He yelled at Trey for not locking the trunk properly, and then he blamed me for not bringing the chest into the room for the night where it obviously would have been safer. I cried. Graypay has never yelled at me before, even when I accidently broke Granny Stephie's special tea cup.

I hate hate HATE Alzheimer's.

This is not my Graypay. Aliens who've taken over people's bodies are nicer than this. Brainwashed characters in movies who are programmed to destroy their countries could take lessons from this man.

Trey was doing his best to calm him down, saying things like, "Jack, we'll get to the police station and they will find whoever took your journals. It was such a beautiful chest, I'm sure when they find only journals inside, and they'll leave it behind somewhere. We can stick around here as long as necessary to find it." I wanted to believe Trey's words, but Graypay didn't even hear him. He wasn't there anymore;

instead we were traveling with a three-year-old temper tantrum trapped inside a seventy-eight-year-old man.

And then my world exploded in a flash of metal against metal and screaming tires, all mingled with the piercing splash of shattering glass. My mind spun; I know that sounds cliché, but my vision actually spun and flipped like an old-fashioned movie filmstrip. Within jumping vision, I saw a face, creased with fear and tears. He was talking, no, yelling that he was sorry, so sorry, he didn't see us. Then he ran back to his car and left. Trey slumped over the steering wheel, bleeding all over his shirt. Graypay leaned against the car door, not moving, and I saw a huge gash on his head.

Panic tastes much like your last meal. I remained panicking until I heard the sirens and knew that help was on the way. The spinning flip of my vision narrowed down to a small circle and then blackness wrapped me with soundless arms and I became as still as Trey and Graypay.

Eddie

Eddie watched from across the street. Easy targets. An old man and two young ones dressed like models in some magazine. Eddie shook his head. *What were they thinking? That they could come to this part of town and not expect to raise a few eyebrows with that car? Cherry!*

He watched as the young man pulled into the gas station and moments later he held his credit card. Franklin Bordeaux III. Even the name had money.

Fewer and fewer opportunities for break and enter jobs because every corner house had a security system. Getting 'round those systems called for equipment and the know-how and Eddie had neither. Back in the day, Eddie could memorize credit card numbers in the minute it took to swipe the card. The customers were never wise to him, they just smiled and fell into the meaningless chit-chat with Eddie's co-worker, Fanny. Man, she could talk! There were days customers would back out of the door without Fanny realizing that they were leaving her mid-story.

Back in the day, he could memorize the numbers. Not now. Now the drinking slowed his mind. Now his hands shook when he even thought of trying to steal the numbers. His hands were shaking now as he watched that car pull into the hotel across the street.

Get a grip, Eddie, he wiped his hands on his jeans. If he timed it right, Eddie could stand a few parking spaces away, grab a bag while they were paying for the room, and no one would even see him. Low-tech. Eddie-style. That car had old locks, the kind Eddie had picked a thousand times. This hotel had security cameras but he knew they didn't work. Nothing worked on this side of town. Nothing but the credit card machines.

Just as he was about to slip across the street to snag something from their open trunk, another customer pulled up. Muttering a curse, he returned to his station at the counter and took a swig of his Coke. If they were spending the night, he could snag something late tonight. It would mean popping the trunk, but for an old car like that, there would be no alarms. Easy as cherry pie!

After his shift, Eddie, walked as casual as anything by the old man's car. It was almost like the old days, except for the sweating palms. His heart jumped when his screwdriver popped the lock in less than ten seconds.

Stupid people, he thought. *Anyone who wanted anything safe should have better locks. It's like they just want me to take that old chest.*

And take it he did. It was heavy. Eddie tried not to think about the fact that it wasn't heavy enough to hold anything like gold or silver.

Damn fool, he laughed. *Not likely to find an old pirate's treasure chest here.*

But it was heavy enough to hold something of value. Eddie had seen the old man touch it back at the gas station. People just don't go touching wooden chests like that unless it's valuable. Eddie remembered the way the old man looked when he touched the box, like he was touching a woman. Real gentle like.

Eddie handled women differently. He shoved the box into his bag and strolled away from the hotel. He kept looking behind him to see if they would come out. No one did. Eddie allowed himself a smile. Beads of sweat glistened on his forehead and upper lip and Eddie wiped them away like an athlete with a gold medal. Breathing a deep sigh, he coasted to the finish line.

"No way!" Stan laughed when Eddie retold his story of the chest. "You ain't never stole nothing in daylight!"

"Man! You don't know me," said Eddie, leaning back in his plastic chair, hoping his nervous twitch didn't reveal that it had been pitch black during his heist, unless you count the light in the parking lot, which made it feel like daylight. "Back in the day…"

"Not a 'back in the day' story," Stan shook his head. "You full of stories."

"Here's the proof, Stan." Eddie patted the wooden chest with his hand. "Here's a treasure chest. I'm like a pirate and I took this here treasure and made it mine. That's the way."

"And you really picked the lock?" Stan asked.

Eddie nodded and took a drink.

Stan touched the chest. "Never seen a box like this. Suppose you are some kind of crazy pirate. You sure drink enough."

"Yeah, and drinks on me after we pawn this stuff."

"How much ya' think?"

"Them folks were from the city. Can tell by the girl's clothes. All fancy and like what you see on TV. No telling what's in there."

"You gonna bust the lock?" Stan asked. Eddie knew he was testing him. He told a whopper story few months back about being the best lock-pick of his day. Truth be told, Eddie hadn't picked a lock in over ten years. Technology and Eddie's nerve had changed. Crow-bar and screwdriver. That was more his style now. *Although it was really no style at all,* Eddie thought.

"No, man, I think I'll do this your way," Eddie smiled. The crow bar was in the other room. By the time Eddie returned, Stan was laughing up a storm. Eddie didn't laugh. Stan *was* the best lock-pick and had neatly opened the chest. Eddie leaned over the table and looked inside.

"Man! You the worst thief! You done stole a box of paper!" Eddie pushed Stan out of his chair, where he continued to laugh and roll on the floor. "What you gonna do with notebooks?"

Eddie picked Stan up off the floor, hauled him to the door and pushed him into the hallway. "I read."

Stan stopped laughing. "Hey, man. I just havin' some fun. I know you read. I seen you read that newspaper every day. Course, you gotta steal it first and if you're nervous sweat runs all the ink." He exploded in a renewed fit of laughter.

Eddie locked the door and turned up the radio when Stan started banging on the door to come back in; his drink was still in there. Eddie had no plans to let him in again tonight. He knew soon enough the landlord would come and make Stan leave and Eddie wouldn't have to get his hands dirty at all.

The notebooks lay in the chest like deadweight. Eddie took another drink, wiped the sweat off his face and took another drink.

Who's more stupid? Me for stealing paper or that old man for thinking notebooks were worth something? Why put these in such a fine wooden chest?

Maybe the chest was worth something. Eddie felt the wood again. Maybe if he had been a boy scout he would know what kind of wood it was, but his mind allowed only the knowledge that it was wood and not a composite material. It was well made, not something store bought.

Crafted with care.

That's what Ma, one of his foster mothers, used to say. She was a lady. Always working on some project - knitting, cross-stitch, painting - but always made the time for her foster kids.

He opened the chest and removed the notebooks. The inside of the chest was lined with an old quilt, the squares small and no two alike. Ma would have loved this box.

Too bad I couldn't have stayed with Ma, thought Eddie as he touched a yellow square of cloth that reminded him of the flowers she kept in the kitchen windowsill over the sink.

Reality, But No TV

Trey

I've watched television all my life - professional viewer, a fan with an opinion, a connoisseur of intense computer graphics - I thought I knew what it would feel like to be in a car accident. All the shows with crashes showed the sparks flying off the road, the screeching tires, and the fantastic acrobatics of the cars as they flip end over end in a spectacular finale with the main characters walk away and the bad guys are dead.

In real life, it's nothing like that. In real life, it comes straight at you while you stomp on the brakes and are paralyzed when you realize that you aren't going to stop in time. The tires slip leaving the screech of the rubber-on-road the only sound filling the gap between heart beats.

The noise of crunching metal was different from the movies: not felt through the mild vibrations of surround-sound speakers, but in the car, in the seatbelt squeezing painfully, and in the steering wheel shaking powerfully, permeated by raining glass like pixie dust on drugs.

It was so fast. It all changed so fast. Graypay was carrying on about the journals being stolen and Alison was crying when it all stopped.

I woke up in the ambulance and was treated for a bump on the head that bled terribly, but left me with only a mild concussion. Small cuts and bruises and sore muscles kept me from sleeping well. That and the beeping machines and nurses who tried not to interrupt my sleep as they drew blood and squeezed my arm with the blood pressure cuff. Did they really think that I was going to sleep through that?

Graypay is in surgery for his injuries and Alison is being treated for some bumps and bruises and possibly a concussion. The television in this room is broken which is just as well; I don't want to see another car crash on a show - ever. It's ridiculous to think they can even replicate the real drama of a crash. Sure, they come close. But why would anyone want to relive that?

Eddie

Stan's laughter resounded off the bare halls, pierced the walls of the staircase and came through the thin glass as he walked down the street towards home, or wherever Stan was calling home these days.

I'm so tired of being embarrassed. Eddie drank down the last of his beer and went the fridge for another. *So sick of people looking at me and seeing right through me, seeing that I'm nothing. I wish I had never been in no foster home. Why couldn't my teachers have taught me to think better? Why didn't no one tell me to go to some trade school? I thought it was so stupid to spend time learnin' something when I could just go out and get a job.*

Those had been Eddie's sweetest years, these few seasons that he made more money than all his buddies from school. Eddie had a studio apartment with a fridge of beer and a table with ash trays built right in. The guys were always welcome at Eddie's because he didn't care if the furniture that came with the apartment was spilled on or what happened to the floor. That place had been a beacon of freedom that so many friends had wanted for a time. Some of those friends, after earning a two-year degree, had found jobs in small businesses where they earned a little more money than Eddie and had health insurance.

Eddie wrote that off. Who needed health insurance? Just go to the free clinic and get meds there. Then he learned that health benefits pay for most of the medications, too, and still he didn't go to school.

When other friends, a few years later, graduated from college, they found real careers with company cars, personal computers, cell phones, and more benefits than Eddie could understand. After graduation, those guys never came around to Eddie's apartment, where the furniture smelled like moldy beer. After losing his job at the car wash, Eddie also lost that apartment. When the landlord told Eddie that he owed the last month's rent plus over $800 for damages, Eddie ran. The law caught up with him during a drug raid on the other side of town and Eddie served two years in jail. The jail offered distance learning classes on the internet, things like finance, foreign languages, computer skills, and business management. Eddie didn't take any of it seriously.

Drinking that second beer down, Eddie stared at the journals. Maybe if he had spent more time studying in jail he wouldn't be working at the gas station. Maybe he could have been the manager at the gas station. But he didn't, he wasn't, and now it was too late.

The dank kitchen light shone through the gloom of the undusted apartment and reflected off the darkened window, catching Eddie's reflection. He stopped pacing and stared. A middle-aged man looked back through deeply wrinkled eyes, gray temples, and a faded hairline, but his heart didn't feel a day over eighteen.

I'll burn them. I'll burn these notebooks. Then if Stan goes and blabs about me stealing papers, there'll be no proof.

That idea charged him a bit, or maybe it was the heady feeling from the beer that added a little pep to his step. Eddie dug out a pack of matches from the clutter on the counter, pulled out a notebook and stood in front of the sink. Page by page, he would burn these until there was nothing left but the chest. He would have to get rid of that. Maybe ol' Chuck at the pawn shop would give him a fair price, maybe enough for another meal. A man can only live so long on beer.

He flipped open to the first page and ripped it out, enjoying the shredding sound, knowing that vengeance was his and he would have the last laugh. Whoever thought that notebooks were treasure would never see these again. That would teach them for putting these in such a chest.

The match caught the page quickly, the flames inched up and ate away all the hand-written words. *So long stupid words. You're no match for fire.*

Match. Fire.

Funny. Eddie laughed.

He dropped the page into the sink and watched it consume the words at the top.

The beginning of wisdom is: get wisdom; at the cost of all you have; get understanding.

Eddie turned the water on and quickly doused the flames. The words screamed from the sink as if burning them would have hurt Eddie as much as the fire destroyed the paper. Those words bit into Eddie's skin, raced through his blood and shouted in his ears.

It was so simple. In a flash, he understood.

His entire life, he had waited for something better, passed the time in poverty hoping for an opportunity that would release him from himself. All the other people in the world, all his buddies from high school who had diplomas, degrees, houses and cars – they all had better beginnings, he reasoned. Families, money, school, jobs. Eddie never had those things in his youth and that was why he still didn't.

But as the fire ate up that old paper, the words ate up that old way of thinking. Just a moment ago, Eddie felt steady on his rocky path to nowhere. Now his face was flushed and the room whirled as if a rollercoaster had snatched his mind and zipped around the track.

The beginning of wisdom is: get wisdom.

Crazy. Simple. Too simple. Is it really like that? Eddie wondered. *I want wisdom so I can get it? No. I can't just suddenly have wisdom.*

But a moment ago he knew this life would always be his life and now he felt something shifting. New possibilities.

Get wisdom. Where?

Frozen to the spot in the tiny kitchen of his apartment, Eddie stared at the water-drenched words which clung to the bottom of the sink. Heat bubbled just under Eddie's skin. Sweat sprang through his pores and he began to tremble.

"I don't want to read anymore. I don't like this." He was alone, but he spoke aloud and that surprised him.

A whisper tickled his heart. *Just read a little more, Eddie.*

That small voice startled him. His muscles tensed and his eyes wanted to look away from the notebook that lay on the counter, missing one page, but his brain read the words.

The beginning of wisdom is: get wisdom; at the cost of all you have; get understanding.

"No. No. No. I can't do this." Eddie pleaded with the whisper.

What are you afraid of?

"What if the words do something to me?" He wasn't comfortable in his skin. Something different, something new was too scary. What would he have to give up? What would he have to suffer?

There is no 'what if', the Whisper answered. *The words* will *change you.*

As much as Eddie wanted to light another match and burn away the whisper, he couldn't. Anger took over; anger at himself for stealing that chest, rage that the notebooks weren't written in Chinese, fury at the Whisper that had entered his mind and planted a seed of wonder.

"I'll show you," Eddie told the Whisper. "I can read these and nothing will happen. I'm not afraid. I'm stronger than some words on a page in a cheap notebook. Watch." With that, Eddie sat down with the notebook, leaving his beer on the counter, and began to read.

And read.

When Eddie closed the last notebook, the sun was up, shining brilliantly through the small kitchen window. Eddie, the gas station attendant, had met Jack Elliott and wanted to be just like him.

Bare Back Jack No More

1948

Jack Elliott

That old man, Jacob, who found me sleeping in the field, took me to the sheriff, who half-heartedly filled out a report, then resumed his nap. When we left the police station, I was angry. Not only had I lost everything, but it didn't seem likely I would have any help from the law in finding that tire-man and my belongings. Jacob pulled his hat snuggly down on his head and gazed out over the small town.

"You a believer, Jack?" he asked.

"A believer of what?"

"Jesus."

I shrugged. "Yeah. I mean I think so, sir."

"True belief doesn't come from what other people tell you," Jacob said. "Even your parents. It comes from what you learn."

"Yes, sir." I wasn't sure what he meant, but Jacob was a big man, and I didn't want to argue and I wasn't going to tell him that the only thing I learned from my dad was the most painful way to land a punch.

"That feller what took your things and hit your head, he's not a believer. He's not trusting the good Lord to provide for him. God saw what happened. He knows you intended to help. If you are a true believer, you'll be fine. Bruised, maybe," he pointed to my head, "but fine." He watched me mull that over. "Understand?"

I sighed. I did. "You're saying that how I respond to being robbed means everything."

Jacob nodded once. "Good man." He motioned for me to follow him. "Anger's what brings a man to troubles. You said first thing you needed was a job. What skills you have?"

"I really don't know for certain," I said. "I'm fair with numbers and can read. I'm good with my hands. Mr. Miller, I worked for him back home, said I was a quick learn. I've some practice on a farm, but no knowledge beyond working hard."

As we talked, Jacob led me back to the General Store, much like the one in Williston, where only the week before, I had strutted the aisles proudly, thinking myself a man of means. Today I had only pocket lint and a growling stomach. Jacob bought some bread and cheese for me. I was very grateful for his generosity. He was right about my anger, but I couldn't make the feeling go away. I could have bought so much more with the money I had, but thanks to that old man, I had to rely on Jacob's charity. I swallowed the bread and cheese along with my bitterness, choking it all down with water.

Jacob told me to ask Mr. Thomas, the General Store owner, if he had any work for me.

"Only on Fridays," Mr. Thomas said. "There's deliveries to some of the homesteads and maybe some cleanin' up 'round the store."

"I can do that," I said, "but one day a week isn't likely to feed me, let alone afford me a place to room."

"True." Jacob thought for a moment. "My wife and I, being long in years, are slowin' down our pace of things. We've a spare room and need of a strong body to do some things. I'll have to talk to Ruthie about a wage – and it likely won't be much, but we can give you a room and meals.

"I can manage that." Anger lost its edge over my thoughts. Having a plan, a job, a place to stay and meals settled me.

Ruthie was happy to have help at the house. I wasn't surprised to learn that their place was the house next door to the church. Jacob was the pastor of the Methodist church. I had joined the Catholic Church with Mr. Howard, but I didn't say anything to Jacob. I figured God would be here too.

Their home was a small bungalow with two rooms upstairs and a kitchen, dining room, a parlor downstairs and an outhouse out the back door. The kitchen had a huge woodstove and a long plank table with benches for seating. Along one wall were shelves with plates, tin cups, jars of canned food and canisters for sugar and flour and such. Miss Ruthie had a neat way about her and her home was the same.

My room needed work, however. The room had been empty since their daughter passed away a few years earlier. They hadn't turned it into a sacred room where all the trinkets their daughter had were kept untouched. Miss Ruth told me that most of her clothes had been given away and she and Jacob encouraged her friends to take some of her favorite belongings.

"Did you keep anything?" I asked.

"We did." She said no more, so I assumed that whatever they kept was no longer in this room. "It will be lovely to have another young person staying here," Miss Ruth changed the subject. "I'm sorry that the room isn't quite ready for you."

"It will be by tonight," I said. "It won't take much. Just a little dusting."

I spent that afternoon banging the dust out of the mattress and pillows, sweeping and making the bed with fresh sheets and a quilt. After supper, Jacob showed me the church and gave me a list of responsibilities. Boredom would not visit me often. The church needed repairs, their small garden was now

115

my small garden, and the barn housed several horses and a few cattle. "That's how I make ends meet," Jacob smiled as he rubbed down a sprite brown mare. "We rent the horse to smaller farmers and sell the beef. Know much about farm animals?"

I shrugged. "Nothing this big. Ma kept chickens, but Pa…" I stopped. Pa had killed them all one night after he came home and found that Ma didn't have supper ready for him. He didn't think it could possibly be because there was no food in the house. "Pa wasn't much of a chicken person." I was careful to not let Jacob know that I had come from a violent family. I didn't want to be that way, but some folks think that where you are from makes who you are. I was on this expedition to prove that wrong.

Jacob probably knew I hadn't been completely honest with him, but he didn't seem to mind. "I hope you like it here, son."

"I have a feeling I will."

CHAPTER 12

June 18
Trey

Both Alison and I had thumping headaches, but we stayed near Graypay. I watched Alison watch her grandfather sleep. It was unlike anything I've ever seen before; like she was being held together with invisible rubber bands and if anything came too close to her and a rubber band broke, she would fall apart like a handful of dandelion fluff scattered carelessly over the floor. The nurse came in to check Graypay and Alison moved against the wall. The doctor tried to list Graypay's injuries so Alison would understand the severity of the situation, but I don't think she heard a word of it. The doctor gave up and spoke to me instead.

It's bad.

He has a broken leg, two cracked ribs, and a serious concussion. A lung was crushed so they had to put him on a ventilator. When I mentioned my thoughts about Alzheimer's, the doctor sighed, "It's not often that a patient his age can recover from these types of injuries. The Alzheimer's will complicate his recovery. If he wakes up."

I know Alison heard that. Her shoulders hunched up higher toward her ears, trying to block out the diagnosis without having to move her arms. She gripped her arms around her chest and tried to lean further away to become one with the drywall, all the while staring at Graypay's ashen face.

It wasn't my fault, but I had been driving. Maybe Alison did blame me. That's why I left the room. The beeping of the heart monitor and the constant stream of nurses in and out of the room made me anxious. I had a concussion, my neck was stiff and sore and I had an all-over ache. Maybe I was aching to go home and be done with this trip. I knew I wanted to be in my own bed and sleep. Then I could to wake up, stay in bed and watch movies until I was so hungry I could barely crawl to the kitchen. Pancakes and ham and fried eggs and coffee. Then back to bed. All this will all be just a dream that I could sleep off and forget when I did finally wake up.

Outside the hospital was worse. An ambulance pulled up and a flurry of ER docs hustled around a shooting victim. As I stood there watching the EMT guys and police and visitors go in and out of the hospital, I remembered what Graypay said that first night of the trip when I was complaining about writing in the journal and told him journals were for girls.

"Nonsense," Graypay laughed. "All the great minds have kept journals."

"Why?" I asked. "Sounds like a waste of paper." *Wow. I am an ass.*

"Only if you don't listen."

I frowned.

118

Graypay continued. "There is a little voice inside that head of yours that needs an opportunity to be heard. If you spend your time in front of the television ignoring the voice, you'll never become who you were meant to become."

"A voice," I said, not believing that Graypay, Mr. Down-to-Earth, heard voices and was encouraging me to do the same.

"A voice," Graypay repeated. "You'll know it when you hear it."

And once again, Graypay was right. As I stood outside the hospital, I heard a voice, "When you become a man, you do things that you need to do, not because you want to, but because they need to be done."

I had left Alison in that hospital room alone because I couldn't stand the look on her face. As I stood on the sidewalk, I knew I had made a mistake.

Following the signs to the cafeteria, I bought two cups of coffee, stuffed my pockets with creamer and sugar packets, snagged a few packages of saltine crackers and returned to the room. Alison was still against the wall, arms folded around her, watching Graypay sleep. I walked to her and handed her the coffee.

"You look cold. Let's sit down together and we'll wait for him to wake up."

Alison's eyes drifted heavily from the bed to the cup of coffee in my hand. I knew I had made a mistake with the coffee. Her chin started to quiver and tears dripped down her cheeks. The rubber bands had broken. She covered her face and sobbed. I quickly set the cups down on the windowsill, and caught Alison as she collapsed into my arms. She was so light, I thought if I squeezed her too hard, she would crumbled into dust. The nurse rushed over and helped me ease her to the floor.

"I don't think she fainted," I told the nurse. "It's just been a really bad day." What day was it anyway?

The nurse checked Alison's pulse anyway until she was satisfied that my non-doctor assessment of Alison's state was accurate. We sat on the floor a long time, my right leg growing numb on the hard tile. When she stopped crying, she slept. An intern and a nurse rolled in a cot for Alison and we carefully lay her on it. She woke for a moment and held my hand tightly.

"He will wake up, won't he?" she whispered.

"You bet." I didn't lie to her. I felt it somewhere deep inside that Graypay would wake up. Even if he didn't, I knew it wasn't a lie. We all wake up; some here, some in the next life.

Alison

I've been sad before. I've felt that gripping in my chest that makes breathing hard. There have been days that I would have liked to stay in bed, hiding beneath the covers; not from monsters under the bed or in the closet, but from the monsters on the street and in school. I saw Graypay cry when Eleanor died. Watching him mourn burned my throat and my lungs. My eyes felt like water balloons stretched too full.

Sadness hurts.

Fear is worse. I know bad days will pass. Rainy days lead to really beautiful spring days. Even at a funeral, there's that little piece of togetherness with loved ones that makes the process just a bit easier.

But a hospital is none of that. I didn't know if he would wake up. I didn't know if Graypay would know me if he did wake up. My Graypay, the tall man that spun me around in the living room like an airplane and took me for walks to the library, on whose knee I sat on every night while he read to me; that man was broken. His skin was suddenly paper-thin. He was so still. Even his breathing was soft and slow.

The nurse told me he was asleep and would be for quite a while. She told me he was broken. I know she was nice and I know she guided me to his room and brought me a chair, but all I could do was stand and watch for his next breath. That's all I needed to see. With each rise of his chest, I knew he was still alive and would be alive, at least for another moment.

I knew I was cold, but I was sweating too. I wanted to lie down and close my eyes and not see any more. If Graypay didn't wake up, I didn't want to either. I was angry and sad and afraid. Mostly I felt trapped: there was nowhere to rest, nowhere to be except there.

And then, Trey was there holding a cup of coffee to me. Coffee. The drink of adults. The warm breakfast beverage of choice, served hot and creamy and sweet with bitter undercurrents. I had waited seventeen years to join my parents and Graypay at the breakfast table with a cup of coffee. That was the only meal we always shared together. Breakfast. Not dinner like most families. Graypay always said that other families did it backwards; that it made more sense to him that families should start the day together instead of end it together. I had only two weeks of coffee with Graypay before we left for this trip. Two weeks of being an adult. Trey was offering me a cup. It wasn't breakfast and I didn't want to be grown up any more. I wanted to curl up on Graypay's lap and listen to him read to me. I wanted to tiptoe into his room after I had a nightmare. That's what this was. No vacation could end so cruelly. No life list of mine ever included this.

I've never fainted from crying before, but I think I did. When I woke up, Trey was sleeping in the chair next to Graypay's bed. His head was against the wall, his mouth open. His face, in sleep, was perfectly relaxed. I don't remember ever seeing Trey's face without that worry crease across his forehead.

Graypay slept too. A hint of pink lit his cheeks and his breathing seemed smoother without the ventilator. I walked to his bed and held his hand. He opened his eyes just a bit and winked at me.

"Morning," I whispered to him, even though it wasn't morning. It was late and dark.

"You hurt?" he asked, his voice gravelly.

"Just a little. No worries."

"Sleep?"

"Me? Yes, I slept." I sniffed and smiled. "Can I get you anything?"

"Box."

"Your journals?"

"The box. Thirty-eight."

"Your journals? Is it important?"

"Yes, Al. You need to find her. The ribbon is hers. Bring her here."

Then I woke up. Again. Or maybe I woke up for the first time. Trey was sleeping in the chair, his head tipped back against the wall, the worry crease still present. Graypay's cheeks did have a hint of color, but he didn't wake when I held his hand and he couldn't have spoken with the ventilator still in place. It had been a dream. I leaned forward and whispered, "I heard you, Graypay."

An Honest Rush

Eddie

Eddie walked quickly along the littered sidewalk. Something in his stomach stirred. It wasn't the chili dog he had for lunch, a lunch he actually paid for. This feeling was deeper than that. Like a storm coming. *I'm becoming a regular barometer*, Eddie frowned. He liked the idea of knowing what was coming, but this feeling didn't tell him exactly what. It was like hearing the tornado siren on a perfectly clear day. Something was coming. Something was changing. He walked quickly to the grocery store, trying to outrun the feeling.

What's the rush? he asked himself. *Slow down.*

But his feet didn't listen to him. His heart continued to race. He had ten dollars left over after his rent was paid; he actually paid his rent on time this month. Ten dollars for a week of food. He could steal some from work, more hot dogs or nachos, but the thought of stealing made him sweat. Holding the shopping basket in his hand, he held the grocer's weekly ad with the other. If he bought all sale items, he could do it. With the sale items, he could possibly stretch ten dollars to last a week.

His stomach rumbled in protest, begging him to grab the apples on the fruit stand and bite into the juicy flesh; eat the apple right in the middle of the store. He turned his back on the fruit. It was too expensive. His mouth watered, his heart pumped harshly in his chest.

When had grocery shopping become such a rush? he wondered.

Eddie took a deep breath and slowed his mind. One thing at a time. Those were Jack's words. One thing at a time. Life rushes at us too quickly. Take it slow, admire the view, live the life you have.

The storm in his mind, powered by his raging heart, stalled just long enough for him to feel in control. One false step and he knew he would be swept away in a torrent of temptation.

Careful now, Eddie told himself. *Careful steps.*

Macaroni and Cheese.

Frozen peas.

Three overly ripe bananas from the discounted rack.

Refried beans. Two cans.

No, he put those back. He could boil a bag of dried beans and have seven servings instead of just one serving for almost the same price.

Bread. Wonder.

Canned tomatoes were four for three dollars. *Is that a good deal*, he wondered? The tag on the shelf told him he would be saving $0.54 a can.

Eddie looked in his basket. That came to almost ten dollars. That wasn't enough food to last him two days. *Maybe a few apples in my coat pockets…no! No. This is it!* He told himself. *Just buy the food and leave.*

He charged for the register and set his basket on the conveyer belt.

"Find everything ok?" the cashier asked Eddie.

He nodded. The knot in his throat tightened. The storm was coming in the form of an emotional breakdown. He looked at the cashier. She was worn out looking, but she smiled as if she didn't have a care in the world. Her name tag read, "Tammi".

Below that was a white button with black letters reading, "Got Prayer?"

Eddie remembered reading in the journals that Jack stopped to pray when things were tough.

That's what I need to do. Maybe God hasn't given up on me. Maybe He will listen and help feed me.

But even as Eddie thought that, he knew it couldn't be possible. Why would God, the Creator of all things, care if Eddie had enough food? Hadn't Eddie sinned enough to assure his place in Hell along with all the other criminals? No, God couldn't care about him.

But God cared about Jack. He could see that in the way Jack wrote about God and all the things God had given to him. Jack wrote about how Jesus healed all those people- the crippled man whose friends tore through the roof and lowered him to Jesus – who told him to stand, pick up his mat and go. Maybe Jesus would see that Eddie had torn through his barrier. Jesus might tell Eddie to take his groceries and go and then Eddie would feel the weight of a week's worth of food in his bag. It was worth a shot.

Eddie closed his eyes. *OK, God. I'm Eddie. I'm a thief. I'm hungry. I'm trying to do right things, but now I don't have money for food. I want to be good. If you help me find food or earn money for food, I will believe in you. I don't know how to be good, so I guess I need help with that too. So, I'm askin' a lot for my first prayer, but Jack believes and I want to believe too. Please help me God.*

"That's nine fifty-four," Tammi said.

Eddie opened his eyes, a little disappointed. A part of him hoped that the food would be free. From his wallet, he took out the four dollars, another two were in his shirt pocket, and the last three were tucked in his sock. He handed her the

126

money, which she gingerly accepted. He collected his bag and change and left the store.

Eddie watched his feet as he walked. The bag of food was incredibly light. He thought of ways to make the food last. Eat once a day. He knew that would never work, but what other choice did he have?

A voice pulled him from his thoughts. Eddie looked up into the eyes of a man who was holding out a book to him.

"Would you like a book?" the man said.

"What?" Eddie asked.

"I'm from the local mission, here passing out New Testaments." He held the book out for Eddie to see.

"Free?"

"I can't charge a man for the Good Book. It has the power to change a man's soul. Can't put no price on that," the man smiled widely, revealing a mouth full of yellow teeth.

"Thank you," Eddie said, taking the book, wishing it was covered with sauce and edible.

The man followed Eddie. "You need help, brother?"

"What?" Eddie asked again.

"You just seem a little lost. You need help?"

"Naw, man," Eddie shook his head.

"I know what you're thinking," the man continued. "You're thinking, How can a man looking so down in the dumps himself offer me help?"

It was only then that Eddie looked beyond the yellow teeth. Long hair in need of a brush, but clean. Old clothes with patches on the knees. The sweater over a button down shirt reminded Eddie of the old men he'd seen on TV, an unshaven, former smoking Mr. Rogers maybe.

"See me?" the man said, holding out his arms. "I'm a changed man. I found redemption and I've been saved."

"And now you pass out free bibles?" Eddie asked.

"Among other things," the man said and held out his hand. "Name's George."

"Eddie." The gesture startled Eddie. Gentlemen shook hands. Eddie was not a gentleman, but he liked the feel of it. His friends didn't shake hands; they punched shoulders. Hard, too.

"See, I know that look you've got," George said. "You've been feeling somethin'."

Eddie's eyes widened.

George jumped and punched Eddie in the arm.

"I knew it man! I knew it! You've been bit by the Good Book."

So much for gentleman, Eddie thought. "This?" Eddie held up the New Testament. "I ain't even read it yet."

"Somethin' got to you, though," George said. "Somethin' got in your gut and is makin' you sick. Just go with it, man. Just go and find what it is and that feeling will grow and start feelin' right."

Eddie looked at the book. "Right now the strongest feeling in my gut is hunger." He held out the meager bag of groceries. "This all I got until next week." That sticky lump in his throat was back.

"Ah, man," George said. "That's tough. I can show you how to get food."

Eddie closed his bag and started to walk away. He'd been in situations like this before. First it was an offer for exactly what you need. Getting it was easy, all you have to do is take it. That's how he got here, to this place of desolation. "No, man. I ain't stealing no more."

"Not stealing," George said. "Earning. Helping others."

"You mean a job?"

"Volunteering. See, there's a place called The Pantry that has shelves and shelves of food. If you need the food, you can go there and they give you some. Not enough for three squares a day, but enough to get you by. Anyway, there are lots of folks that don't want hand-outs."

Eddie nodded in agreement. He may be hungry and poor, but he would never be a charity case.

George continued, "So they came up with a plan. You deliver food to some folks that can't leave their house and you earn the food."

"So it's like working for food."

"Yeah! There's people who ain't got legs or some can't see and it's near impossible for them to work and earn money and even more difficult to get around. Folks deliver bags of food to them. Sit and visit sometimes. Pray even."

Eddie's heart twisted until he almost cried out in pain. Prayer. He had never prayed with another person. The prayer he spoke just a few moments ago at the checkout line was the first one since he was a kid and prayed to God to give him roller blades. To sit and visit? What did he have to say to anyone? "I don't think so," Eddie said starting to walk away. "Thanks for the offer."

George didn't argue or try to insist that Eddie try. Eddie was thankful for that. He just shrugged and held out his hand again to Eddie. "Your choice, man. Pantry's over on Walnut between Wood Avenue and Pine Street, 'case you change your mind."

The book, the New Testament, was small with print and delicate pages seemed a disappointment. Jack had mentioned the Bible in his journals, referred to verses with great reverence. As Eddie read Jack's journals, he longed to read beyond the few verses Jack copied. Years ago when Eddie attended church with one of his foster parents, he remembered the gold-edged pages and ornate lettering in the bible at the front of the church. It was on a pedestal before the altar for parishioners to read when they visited the chapel. The church was just a few blocks from his foster home, so Eddie would go there sometimes and just sit. The priest had expressed hope in Eddie's future, but Eddie only wanted the quiet. His whole life was one noise after another. His mother cried a lot. The first foster home had three babies who cried. School was always busy. Even in his dreams, the clamor didn't go away. The church was tranquil.

Funny, I haven't thought of that church since I left that home. Now with the New Testament in hand, it all came flooding back. He remembered that if he sat real still with the book from the pew on his lap, no one bothered him. They thought he was praying, but he wasn't. He was just soaking in the silence as if it were a hot spring bath, easing all the aches and pains of life.

Eddie didn't know how to read then, but he loved to look at that book. It was rich looking and he was sure that if he could read the words, he would have a family again. That foster mother never thought to read the words to Eddie. Maybe she couldn't read either.

The little Bible in his hand didn't have gold-edging or fancy first letters at the beginning of each chapter, but he knew the words would be the same. Something about the words pulled at his curiosity. But something stronger made him want to drop the book into a puddle and run. If he opened this book, he knew his life would change. Did he want that? He had seen people at the shelter reading their Bibles and smiling or sometimes crying, but they were still in the shelter. Wasn't God supposed to care for the people who believed in Him? He knew the Bible held words that changed people and he wasn't sure he wanted to be like them. They seemed drunk all the time; praising God for all their sufferings. One woman at the Soup Kitchen prayed over her meal, thanking God for teaching her humility and for bringing her there for the food. Eddie wouldn't thank God for humility. It was not a gift he wanted.

He flipped the book open and read a quick verse:

"Come to me, all you who are weary and are carrying heavy burdens, and I will give you rest."

"Damn," Eddie muttered, and then added an even quieter apology to God for swearing while holding a Bible. He didn't know for sure, but he was sure that was against the rules. He closed the book and turned the corner, nearly bumping into Lou.

"Hey man," Lou said, smiling when he recognized Eddie. "You seen Stan?"

"Nah," Eddie closed the tiny New Testament and tucked it into his pocket before Lou would notice. If there was anyone Eddie knew that could spread news faster and make it sound as horrible as possible, it was Lou.

"Whachya got?"

Too late, Eddie sighed. "A book,"

Lou laughed, "Been to Heritage Market? I seen some guy out there earlier passing out Bibles."

Eddie laughed too and held up his grocery bag.

"You mean," Lou glanced at Eddie's pocket like it that little Bible might shoot out flames and burn him to a crisp on the spot, "you took one?"

"He was handing them out."

"But," Lou glanced around and leaned in, "You don't want people talkin."

"About what?"

"About you becoming one of them hypocrites," Lou nearly spat out the words. "One of them folks what do whatever they want but tells you that you can't do what you want. Church-goers what nearly pluck you off the sidewalk on Sunday mornin' when they's late for the sermon."

"Just a book, man," Eddie quickened his step.

"That ain't no book," Lou yelled after Eddie as he continued to walk away. "That book will lose you all your friends. Don't become one-a-them, Ed! Just throw that thing away."

Eddie waved, but didn't say anything.

"You going to Fred's for poker this week?"

"Yeah, maybe."

Lou shook his head, knowing that a 'maybe' from Eddie was really a 'no'.

"Throw it out!" Lou called. "And tell Stan I need my money. Better yet, give the book to Stan and maybe he'll pay me back."

Once he was safe in his apartment, Eddie knew that Lou's loose lips would be telling everyone that he had seen Eddie with a Bible.

It bothered Eddie that Lou's opinion of what he read bothered him. Maybe he's a friend worth losing, Eddie thought as he set the bag of groceries on the table and pulled the New Testament out of his pocket. If he's a friend worth losing, he's no friend at all.

October 1949 - 1953
Jack Elliott

Almost seven months later, I had enough money for a train ticket to Washington State, and enough money left over for food along the way and a good start. It was December, though, and Jacob and Ruthie needed me around the house until spring, at least. I didn't argue. I loved helping them. By the time I did leave the following May, they had enough wood cut for two more winters, the garden was started and the church's roof was as solid as a rock.

Leaving Jacob and Miss Ruthie was more difficult than leaving my own home. They treated me like a man, gave me great responsibilities, and loved me – and I them. I said good-bye to Mr. Thomas and his wife. I knelt quietly in church the evening before I left in humble thanks. I left Ohio so I wouldn't become my father. Thanks to Six-String Sam and Ice Box Bill, I didn't hurt anyone through my anger. Thanks to Jacob and Ruth, I had a good reputation and a peace in my heart that had never been there before. This little town and this little church would always be a part of me.

I memorized the way the roof slanted above Jacob's podium, the way the pews were never comfortable, the dark piney knots in the walls that still oozed pitch. This place was always quiet, even during the Sunday services when folks respectfully listened to the readings, the comments on the scripture. It was the reverence for the Holy One that preserved my belief in God. In the Catholic Church in Ohio, the feeling of the building with the incense permeating the woodwork, the presence of God was felt in the awe-inspiring crucifix over the altar and the bowed heads. I carried that with me to this little church, which smelled of pine-pitch and beeswax candles, the same expectation I had at the church back home: that if I was here, God heard me more clearly. I knew that God could hear me anywhere I went, but I like the idea that if I came to his home, His heart was closer. There was no kneeler in front of the altar here, but I knelt anyway. Seemed necessary for the amount of praying and requests I had.

Miss Ruthie packed some bread and beef jerky for me. Jacob had purchased a canteen just like the soldiers used. I would have liked to stay there a little longer, but my restless heart didn't want to leave a place because I had to. I wanted to miss the places I left behind; feeling homesickness was good. I knew I now had two homes to which I could return and neither one was my biological family.

In my wisdom, I divided my money up and kept a little in my shoe, a little in my wallet, and the rest in a small pocket that Miss Ruthie had sewn inside my shirt. My luggage was now a small backpack with one complete change of clothes, a bible, and a notebook. I felt stronger and more prepared for the possibilities.

I made it to Seattle without any trouble. Within two days, I had found a place to stay and a job. I imagined that I would find work on the wharf, Seattle being near the water. Instead, the only work available at that time was at a dairy farm, feeding and milking cows and helping to birth calves. The family there wasn't quite as peaceable as Jacob and Miss Ruthie, so when an opportunity for a job in the dining car of a train came up, I took it.

I rode between Seattle and Los Angeles, serving coffee, tea, mixed drinks and little crustless sandwiches. During a two-day vacation in Los Angeles, I stumbled into a job at a movie studio as a guard for one of the lots. It was a short-term job, lasting only a month, but I saw movie stars and directors in all their glory and I saw them behaving badly. Beyond the fleeting moments when the actors and directors came through my gate, the job was pretty dull. I had imagined that the air in Hollywood would be electric. From my little post, I decided that all the excitement took place behind walls, in sound studios, or on location.

After Hollywood, I went to Wyoming and hiked for the summer. I bought supplies, equipment, and food and disappeared for almost five months. After living among busy cities and train cars, then Hollywood, I wanted to immerse myself into nothing. I was wrong. The nothingness I sought could not be found. Instead of people to tend with, I had trails and weather and hunger and cold. My challenges were different, but equally fulfilling. I emerged in late September in Northern Wyoming stronger than ever.

I met a Park Ranger, Henry, as I looked for work. He hired me on the spot after learning that I had just walked out of the woods. Now I was one of two winter residents at a lodge in the Rocky Mountains, tending the property and documenting buffalo and wolf counts, which to my surprise was more about counting piles of poop. During the summer months, I led walks on the trails, answered questions about the animals, and directed activities. I learned to track animals, understood their patterns and habits. I saw parts of Yellowstone National Park that most folks don't know exist.

At the beginning of fall, just before my third winter at the National Park, a letter from Miss Ruthie came, asking me to come home. Five days later, we buried Jacob. I stayed with Miss Ruthie through that winter and that was when I fell in love.

Little One

October 1953
Jack Elliott

In town, a few months before Jacob passed away, a fire had claimed three buildings and eight lives. An entire family had died trying to put out the flames and save their few possessions. There was only one survivor. Just one. The tiniest little thing I've ever seen.

Miss Ruthie didn't know her name; the family had moved here from China shortly after I left, and the little girl was born about two years ago, nobody knew exactly when. Jacob and Miss Ruthie took her in after the fire. There was no one else. Town folk didn't feel comfortable taking in a foreign child, didn't want to feed another mouth, didn't want to clothe another child. Miss Ruthie didn't hesitate.

When I first came back, Little One, as we called her, wouldn't come near me. She hadn't uttered a sound since the fire a few months before. I asked Miss Ruthie if she was concerned about that.

"No. Not yet. She was probably just starting to talk in her own language when her family was killed. Now she's here with us, listening to our speak, and taking it all in." Miss Ruthie wiped Little One's mouth. "Besides," she continued, "sometimes children stop talking after their folks die. I did."

"What happened?"

"I was four or five when they were killed during a storm. I had older brothers and a younger sister, so it wasn't so bad for

137

me. This Little One has no one." Miss Ruthie's eyes looked red again, tears surfaced very easily for her since Jacob's death.

I changed the subject. "Tomorrow I'll go to the post office. Maybe someone has written back." That had been Jacob's plan. When they took in Little One, he sent letters to all his contacts in the ministry, asking them all if there were any families who would be interested in adopting a little Chinese girl. It had been three months and no word yet.

"You haven't named her," I said to Miss Ruthie a month after Jacob died.

"She already has a name. I just don't know it."

I looked at Little One and felt something behind my ribs pound. I'd never spent any time around babies or toddlers, and I was intrigued by the way she could do most everything and yet be so tiny. She walked and used a cup and played with a little doll Ruthie made her. Mannerisms of a lady all packed into a petite body. Her black hair shone with iridescent colors as if God had poured every color imaginable into each strand. With eyes that shone like polished stone and skin unmarked by life, she was more of a porcelain doll than a little girl. "We'll have to name her. We can't just call her Little One."

Miss Ruthie looked over at the little one. "What name would fit?"

"Little One certainly fits, but it has to be a name she can grow up with." I watched her play with a doll Miss Ruthie had sewn up for her from old scraps of cloth.

"You'll think of something," said Ruthie. Then I understood why Miss Ruthie hadn't named her. For the same reason you don't name farm animals. This sweet Little One wasn't going to be staying with her forever. In going through the process of giving her a name, she would become more of Miss Ruthie's heart and then the separation would be more painful. Having a nameless child helped her keep her distance. She had already lost her daughter and now Jacob. She knew I wouldn't be staying forever, and that Little One couldn't.

"You want *me* to name her? Isn't that a bad idea?"

Laughing, Ruthie scolded me. "She's not a cow that children name and then won't eat when the steaks are on the table. She's a child."

I pleaded my case. "Then you should name her. You're already a mother. Doesn't naming children come naturally?"

Ruthie peeked around the corner at Little One as she sat on the floor with a few toys. "You can't see it because she's so quick, but every time you look away from Little One, she looks at you. When you look at her, she looks away."

I glanced at Little One and saw her quickly look away. "Why does she do that?"

"Only God knows for sure, but I would venture a guess. She likes you."

I moved behind the table, keeping an obstacle between me and Little One. "I don't know how to care for a child."

"I've never asked about your growing up years," said Ruthie gently, "and I won't ask now unless you want to tell. I figure that you've been through some rough patches and think that's why you don't know how to care for children."

Remaining sternly focused on the floor, I couldn't meet her eyes. She was right.

"Jack. In the time you have been here, I've not seen an ounce of displaced anger. You are kind and generous and gentle. This Little One has lost everything. She needs a young someone to care for her."

Still shaking my head, I was starting to feel some of my displaced anger surface. "You don't understand Ruthie. I don't know anything about little girls. I'm twenty-one. I'm not married. Who in their right mind would think I would be a good parent?"

"I do." She stood up, a feat which took more effort than it did three years ago, and pointed at me with her knitting needle. "I've seen you with the children at church, the way they flock to you as if you were the Good Shepherd himself. Let God take control of this. Open your heart to that Little One and see what happens. I believe that God has brought you here for a reason."

"Ruth—" I started.

She held up her hand. "I'll not force this on you, but I have a strong feeling that I'm right. Pray about it, Jack."

I took Little One with me the next day when I went to the post office so Miss Ruthie could have some rest; Little One only came because I carried her on my shoulders. Miss Ruthie said she was smiling.

Miss Ruthie also gave me a list of items to purchase from Mr. Thomas. It was our first outing together and I was nervous. Miss Ruthie laughed at me when I asked her about little girls and outhouses and what to do if she sneezes.

"Being a guardian to a child is a gift from God. When they have to go, you help them. When they sneeze, use your handkerchief. If she falls, pick her up and dry her tears."

I could feel my shoulders grip my neck. "That doesn't help. You're a woman. Parenting comes natural to you."

Miss Ruthie waved her finger at me. "Men are parents, too. Don't you *ever* forget that. You love that Little One, Jack Elliott. You can't fool these old eyes. I've seen the way you watch her play, the way you smile at her. She's got a hold of your heart. You just treat her like the gift from God she is. Everything else will fall into place."

Little One rode on my shoulders all the way into town. I pointed at all the things I could see and told her the English words for them. She still hadn't spoken, but Miss Ruthie assured me that she would. In her own time, she would find the words.

Mrs. Thomas was thrilled to see Little One and offered her a peppermint stick, which quickly dissolved into a sticky mess in my hair.

"Set her down, Jack, before she turns your head into a sugar helmet," Mrs. Thomas teased. "And come on ova' here. My girls are all grown now, but I saved a few of them dresses." In a basket behind the counter were six dresses. Holding one up to Little One, Mrs. Thomas exclaimed, "Why, you're just a miniature! I'll have to take these in and hem them up good."

The little one tugged on my hand. A look in her eye was new, she wanted something. I knelt next to her.

"Mini?" she said.

"That's right," I smiled so wide I thought my heart would jump right past my teeth. "Mini. Mrs. Thomas will make the dresses fit you." I looked at her, then Mrs. Thomas. Her face was as excited as mine.

"Is that her first word?" she asked, whispering as if a loud voice would spoil the magic of the moment.

"It is. I think that will make a perfect name."

Minnie.

CHAPTER 13

The Car Lot Guy

June 19

Trey

I knew Alison would feel better after a shower and a change of clothes. Or, at least, I hoped a shower would wash away her worries about Graypay, but we had only borrowed scrubs from the hospital to wear. Our luggage was still in the car. We looked like asylum run-aways in our hospital garb, bandages and bruises.

Officer Decker drove us to the station to fill out a formal report and Alison worked with him and a computer program to try to recreate the face of the man that hit us. Every now and then I glanced over at her and felt my insides twist as her face reddened.

"The lips were thinner. Maybe not so wide. No, that's not right. The nose was longer…" and on and on she tried. By the time I had completed my paperwork, Alison was near tears.

"Let's stop for a while," Officer Decker said. "We'll give you some time to think about it."

"I just can't remember the rest of his face. But those eyes," she pointed to the screen, "those are almost perfect."

"Let's go get our luggage," I suggested. "Can we get to the car? Our luggage and everything is in there."

"The lock-up is just around the corner. Dave mans the office there." The officer handed me the keys and I signed a paper stating that the officer had given me the keys. Seriously? One more piece of paper to fill out? We had already filed a formal report about the hit and run, which required us to go to the police station; where Officer Decker wrote our names and addresses on a half dozen slips of paper and wrote out what we remembered from the accident. I had a dent on my finger from gripping the pen so hard.

The office checked my signature against my driver's license. "Here you go, Franklin."

"It's Trey."

"What?" the officer asked.

"I go by Trey. Franklin Bordeaux, the Third. Trey. It's French for three."

The officer shrugged and handed me the keys. Graypay's keys. The set with the hand-braided key chain Alison made for him. Two keys clinked together, one to the car that would never see the pavement again and the other to the chest, which was lost. "Dave will point you to it. Officer Decker will meet you at the lot to drive you back to the hospital."

I expected to find a large lot with all kinds of cars waiting for hauling or forensic investigation. Instead I found I square of asphalt large enough for ten cars, and currently holding only two. There was no need for Dave-the-lot-man to even be in his small booth, but that didn't stop him from first calling the

144

officer we had just left to approve the removal of our luggage from the car for which we had keys and paperwork.

"Right." Dave said, hanging up the phone. "Officer Decker said you are approved to search the car."

"We aren't here to search the car. It's ours," I said. "We just need our luggage."

"Right," Dave said. "I should have the keys here."

"I have keys." I held up the keychain with two keys clinking.

"Right, then." Dave struggled to hold on to his authority of the two-car lot. "Your car is parked second from the end," he pointed to the nearly empty lot.

I glanced back at Alison and shrugged. She giggled. A first hint of any happiness since the accident. "Thanks. Wouldn't have found it without your help." I meant it as a joke, but Dave the car-lot guardian beamed with pride.

As we neared the car, Alison grabbed my hand. "Trey, how did we even survive?"

I didn't know.

Alison hung back as I unlocked the truck and pulled out our suitcases. Officer Decker met us there a few minutes later and drove us to a building across the street from the hospital. My stomach dropped and I knew I was in trouble. "Um. This is a hotel," I said, knowing I was stating the obvious, but shocked that Officer Decker didn't take us across the street.

"Can't stay overnight at the hospital unless you are a patient. You both have been discharged. You can walk over whenever you want, shower and rest between visits to your grandfather." He opened his door and pulled the lever that opened the trunk. "You're in luck. They have one room left."

"But, we, um…" How could I say this? "We aren't…I'm…"

Officer Decker laughed. "I know. The room is paid for by your mother," he nodded his head to Alison. Turning to me, he

145

gave me a stern look. "I was told to remind you of the promise you made. If you break that promise, I've got handcuffs right here and the jail isn't far away."

Officer Decker was clearly enjoying my discomfort, but I also knew Mrs. Elliott to be a woman of her word. I assured him that the promise was still in effect and wouldn't be broken for anything. I climbed out of the car quickly and pulled the collar of my scrubs away from my neck, as the heat of scrutiny from Mrs. Elliott through Officer Decker's glare brought on cold sweats.

Alison

"There isn't much here," Trey commented as we spread the contents of Graypay's luggage on one of the beds in our hotel room.

I nodded. "Graypay traveled light. He lives light."

Completely unlike me. My life was heavy with expectations, plans and cluttered with the trinkets of every moment I thought had been important: movie ticket stubs, dried flowers, my baby blankets. None of those things mattered to me now. I would gladly hand them all over to the angel of miraculous healing if Graypay would just wake up.

A million thoughts like that hummed heavily between my ears, but talking was too hard. Took energy. Too many things had happened. We had driven through too many places. I'd spent my entire life chewing my way out of Chicago and now I couldn't separate all the places I've been in the past few days. The world was supposed to show me differences, new horizons, new sun sets.

Was this the adventure I'd always wanted? Didn't the great stories all have moments of tension, scary moments? Those were stories, safely pressed between the covers of a book, not seeping into my dreams and hopes for what my life would be. My life was not supposed to be a tragedy. There had been only family times and school and good books. Now there was a hospital and beeps from a machine and a pounding in my head that wasn't eased by the pain killers and a growing sense that this was all my fault.

If I hadn't made that stupid life list, Graypay and I would be sitting in our apartment drinking a cup of coffee and sharing a good book. Instead, I was far away. Graypay was further away, and I was sifting through his personal effects. This event was nowhere to be found on my life list.

I discovered many things about Graypay just from his luggage. First, he folded clean clothes as well as dirty clothes. His luggage looked professionally packed with shirts and pants folded like origami: neat squares and without any wrinkles. Second, he was a boxer guy. I *really* didn't need to know that. Aside from the clothing and bathroom items, Graypay didn't keep any mystery clues in his bag.

Trey tried to fold everything back into the suitcase as neatly as Graypay had, but not everything fit. We finally settled on doing what we could and hung the remaining clothes in the closet.

"Sorry, Alison," Trey said as he sat down. "I thought we would find something."

"I did too."

"Even his wallet has no clues. Just his license, health insurance card and cash. The picture of you is great, by the way. Who is this?" he asked, holding out a frayed snapshot.

"Granny Stephie."

"You look like her." Trey tucked the pictures back in the wallet and locked it inside the suitcase. "Even the receipts are just from the last few days."

"He doesn't carry anything extra with him," I told him. "Baggage, he calls it."

"Everyone has baggage," Trey said.

"Sure, but not everyone is like Graypay," I reminded him.

"True," Trey said. "Well, so much for our detective work."

We went back to the hospital and sat near Graypay, both of us absorbed in our thoughts, mine marching steadily with the beeps of the heart monitor.

Trey had dozed off in the chair. With Graypay's bible in hand, I went in search of the hospital chapel. I wasn't alone in the softly lit room. Several others sat in the stillness of the room. There was no crucifix or cross, no marking of any kind to show that this room was reserved for those seeking God other than the Chapel sign on the door. But I knew. He was everywhere, but especially in the places where people seek him.

Eddie

Eddie took a different way home. It was as if he were a food addict succumbing to a huge bowl of ice cream or an AA graduate rushing to his meeting instead of to the bar for a fix. He smiled as he felt that old need, the old desire quicken his step. It wasn't a drink or a smoke that drove him. It was silence. He craved silence and he knew it wasn't going to hurt him; it wouldn't hold him back.

The need for silence drove him to the oldest building on the north end of town. Sts. Peter and Paul Cathedral. The doors were open. Inside, a few old ladies sat quietly with their eyes either closed or gazing at the crucifix. Eddie didn't want anyone to ask him to leave because he didn't look like he belonged. He didn't want to scare the women. He knew he was tall and large and sloppy and therefore intimidating.

Huh, he thought, *I used the word 'therefore' in my thoughts. Interesting.*

He quietly walked to a pew in the back and opened the New Testament from George.

No, Eddie thought, *Jack would never sit in the presence of the Lord.*

He pulled down the kneeler in front of him and assumed a prayerful position. The posture felt strange. Too formal, but he remained on his knees, knowing - no, hoping - that in the weeks and months to come, a formal posture would feel more comfortable. He remembered the kneelers from his youth, how he didn't use them to kneel, but stood on them to see the altar better. If the pew wasn't full, he used the kneeler like a balance beam. All those Sundays at church, all the prayers he heard but didn't listen. Eddie wondered if maybe he would have turned out better if someone had taught him to pray the words or had shown him the words in the book.

He had come seeking the silence he enjoyed when he was a child, soaking it in and breathing deeply the air that didn't vibrate with the bass of nearby stereos or carry the resonance of anger.

It is good, but it's not enough. He missed out on the prayers years ago, but he had enjoyed the peaceful feel of them.

Another piece fell into place.

Eddie had stolen Jack's journals. The journals led him to pray and not two minutes later he was handed a bible and given a solution to his food problem. Now he sat in church. Eddie looked up and allowed the tears of joy and shock and love to roll freely down his face.

You heard me. And you answered.

August 1954
Jack Elliott

"Jack-Jack," I heard Minnie's voice just inches from my face. The sun was far from rising. Now that she could use the thunder pot during the night, saving me from extra laundry, she found a new excuse to wake me. Tonight's reason for sleeplessness? "Jack-Jack, there's a goat under my bed."

This was a new one. "A goat? How do you know it's a goat?"

"I hear it goating."

"Have you been feeding Mr. Simmons goat again and it followed you home?"

She giggled. "No."

"Did you hide Ruthie's jelly jars under your bed and the goat crawled under there to gobble them up?"

"No!" she laughed again.

"Then what is a goat doing under your bed?"

"He wants you to take us outside for star stories." She pulled my hand and I groaned.

"Minnie, I'm tired. Can we do star stories this weekend? I have to work with Mr. Thomas tomorrow."

"But the sky is ready," Minnie said.

I couldn't say no to a ready sky. With pillows and blankets, Minnie and I snuck down to the kitchen without waking Ruth and slipped out the back door to our spot in the field behind the house. Minnie lay next to me with her little head on my arm.

"I'm ready," she announced. "What did the stars see today?"

"Today they saw a beautiful mountain far away from here. It's not a normal mountain like the mountains we see. This mountain is called Ice Mountain, even though it's not made of ice. It's filled with tunnels and caverns that glimmer with crystals. You see, Ice Mountain was created at the very beginning of time, and was so beautiful that anyone who even caught a glimpse of its glimmer would want to travel there and take just a small piece, and forever remember the moment they saw perfection. For many years, that's what happened.

"But when news of the beauty of the mountain spread and people heard of Ice Mountain, the idea of having a piece of it became the only thing people could think of; even the smallest crystals would satisfy. It didn't matter to them that their token was tiny; the journey was what they loved.

"The beauty of the crystals became so well known that the kings and queens all around the world sent explorers to the mountain to bring them back a piece of the mountain. What the kings and queens didn't know, was that the crystals in the mountain were free to anyone who wanted one, but they had to come to the mountain and select a crystal for themselves. When they sent other people to select a crystal for them, that crystal belonged to whoever selected it. No matter what the kings and queens did to protect their purchased crystals, the crystals always returned to the people who plucked them out of the mountain."

Minnie interrupted. "Was it magic?"

"No. It was the purpose of Ice Mountain that anything taken from there, belong to that person. God made that

153

mountain to pull people away from where they were born and out into the world. Some people had to travel very far. Other people lived closer to the mountain so it was an easier journey, but just as wonderful. Those who did make the journey were not only rewarded with the token of a crystal, but the knowledge they gained during the trip. The things they saw, the smells that left prints on their minds, the feel of the air surrounding the mountain; that all left a mark on that person. That's how the crystal knew who it belonged to. When a human hand touches the crystal for the first time, the crystal remembers it and always returns to it. It's not magic. It's love that makes the crystal return to the person who selects it."

"Did everyone go to the mountain?"

"No. Some people never even saw it. Others saw the mountain but thought that the journey would be too hard, so they didn't even try.

"The stars remembered when some people began the journey to the Ice Mountain and couldn't make it. Those people found different jewels that were only meant for them, and they never would have found them if they had made it all the way to the Ice Mountain.

"Today the stars saw Ice Mountain and knew that it had been mistreated. With airplanes and trains making the journey too easy, the crystals are being taken by people who haven't made the journey the way God intended. The crystals are still being taken and cherished, but the journey has been lost.

"Stars know how important the journey is. They know that without a journey, people can no longer appreciate the crystals. If the crystals are taken for granted and found too easily, someday soon, the Ice Mountain will no longer exist.

"Today the stars had seen enough. Some people think that the stars are just big balls of gas in outer space, or little lights in the sky put there just for decoration. But, did you know what the stars are actually guardians of all things precious?"

Minnie wiggled in closer. "Like the Ice Mountain is precious."

"And so is the journey that leads people to the Ice Mountain. So today the stars decided to move the Ice Mountain."

"Where?"

"I don't know. It's a secret."

Minnie rubbed her nose. "Then how will people find the mountain?"

"Well, they will have to make the journey. The stars will show the way, but people will have to start looking at the stars again. The journey must be made with their feet on the ground and all on their own."

"That's a sad story, Jack-Jack."

"I know. That's the story the stars are telling tonight."

CHAPTER 14

Cigar Boxes and Sherlock Holmes

June 20ᵗʰ

Trey

I was too nervous to stay at the hotel. Visions of what Alison's mother would do to my reputation stoked nightmares of law suits and jail time, even though I was totally innocent. Instead of losing more sleep, I left a note for Alison saying that I was going to the hospital to sit with Graypay. The nurse brought me the most comfortable folding chair she could find and with a pillow wedged between my head and the wall, I slept.

When I woke, I had a crick in my neck, a painful rumble in my gut and a headache left over from the concussion. Alison, however, had showered, visited the cafeteria and waited for me to wake as she sipped coffee and ate a bagel. Something had filled her eyes with a familiar gleam, almost as though she had breathed in helium and was tethered to her chair – today if a band holding her broke, she would have lifted off the ground and floated happily away like a stray carnival balloon.

"You look better," I commented, feeling the cotton-dry of my mouth. I knew my hair was sticking up. Alison glanced at it and smiled.

"I brought you breakfast," she pointed to a second cup of coffee and bagel. "I figured it out." She leaned forward. "Graypay planned this trip to be my present. It was a gift from my life list: a cross-country trip, number seventeen. Graypay knows I've read mysteries for years. He said, 'Thirty-eight'."

"Does that mean something to you?" Because it meant nothing to me. She was rambling on like an over-caffeinated lawyer, giving me all the details and no foundation.

"My life list. Number thirty-eight," she said as if I was supposed to remember that crazy list she kept. "With all the mystery novels I've read, I've always wanted to solve a real mystery."

"And the ribbon he mentioned?" I asked. "We didn't find a ribbon in his suitcase. Would it be in the journals?"

"Why would he put all the clues in the journals for me?"

"To *give* you the clues?" Duh! But based on the look on her face, she thought I was the one missing the big picture.

"No way!" Alison scooted forward, smiling as if I was her Watson and the missing piece was so elementary it was preschool fodder. "Graypay would want it to be as real as possible. He never put all his eggs in one basket. He...he wouldn't leave the clues easy to find. That's no mystery. That's a scavenger hunt."

"Where else can we look?" I asked. "We've been through the luggage and the trunk."

"He said to find the box, but he didn't mean the journal box. Trey, will you go back to the car and search it? I mean really search it. Look in the glove compartment, the console, under the seats, anywhere you can think of that he may have hidden it."

I didn't want to go back to that car. Looking at the eagerness on her face, I caved. "What am I looking for?"

"A cigar box. It was on his dresser for years. It's where he kept all his pictures and little trinkets. I didn't see it after he packed."

"And it wasn't in his luggage. So you think that maybe he hid it in the car somewhere."

"Maybe. It's all I can think of. It's the only thing that he kept track of all these years. The clue we need has gotta be in the car."

Finding the cigar box was not easy. I had to take a cab to the police yard where the car was stored. The insurance company hadn't made it there yet to declare it totaled and have it sent to the wrecking yard. A nice woman with a pierced nose and black lipstick glanced at my I.D. and gestured with her head in the general direction of the lot.

Officer Decker helped me search the wreckage for the cigar box.

I finally understood the terms I had heard all my life: twisted metal, riding on the wings of angels, miracle. Maybe the St. Christopher medal hanging from the rear-view mirror really did save Alison and me. Maybe the statue of Jesus that Graypay had cemented to the dashboard did give us a "get out of death" card.

"Not likely that everything will still be in the box," he said. "With a crash like this, I'm sure that it was smashed and dumped all over the car."

"I don't even remember seeing a cigar box," I said. "I'm hoping that's because it's somewhere safe."

The passenger door still wouldn't open. The firemen at the scene had carefully pulled Graypay out the window. Broken glass was sprinkled on the seat, and floor like confetti. I reached through the window and under the seat coming face-to-face with a large blood stain, Graypay's blood, on the vinyl. Jammed under the seat, and protected by a barbed wall of glass, was a black bag. Dusting it off, I unzipped it and pulled out a slightly crushed cigar box.

"Found it."

"What's inside?" Office Decker asked.

"Don't know."

"Must be important."

"Must be." I wouldn't open it. That was for Alison to do.

After all that, Alison took the bag and held it in her lap. "Thank you."

She didn't notice my newly bandaged fingers and she didn't know it had cost me $83.00 in cab fare. "You're welcome," I said, surprised to realize that I really was happy to have found it for her, despite the cost to my wallet and fingers.

She didn't open the box. Just sat there with her eyes closed. When she finally opened her eyes, she smiled at me. "Thank you for finding this. It must have been difficult," she looked at my bandages.

"Not at all." I meant it.

She took a deep breath. "I need your help."

"To go home?" I asked hopefully.

"No. We need to find someone and bring her here. Graypay needs to see her."

I looked at Graypay. "He told you that?"

"Years ago," her voice was rough with emotion, "when I watched all my friends go on vacations and we stayed home, all the weekends that I worked at the deli instead of going out with my friends, I was very angry about my life. Graypay said that he understood. He said that every life started out in a family way, moved to a free way, and then slowly settled to a family way again. He said that there was nothing I could do about changing my life then, but that I should make plans for when I could leave home and live my life the way I wanted. 'Plans are nothing, but planning is everything', he said."

"That sounds like him," I said, glancing at the shell of the man in the hospital bed.

Alison didn't look at him. "He helped me see that I needed to have dreams – wild and wonderful dreams of what I wanted my life to be. He showed me his life list. He made it years ago, before he met my grandmother. It guided him."

"Did he do everything on his list?" I asked. "Is this a 'finish what I've started' thing?"

"He did do most, and no, we don't have to do something on his list. The list is more goal-oriented than outcome oriented. Anyway, this trip was my present. I wanted to see the world," her voice slipped and she glanced at Graypay and all the machinery keeping him alive. "Graypay always warned me that when I finally did get out and see the world, I would see it for what it really was and that I probably wouldn't like what I found. That second part to my present..." She stopped talking. I could see her jaw tighten as she fought off an attack of tears.

"The mystery," I said.

She held the box up for me to see. "Graypay has Alzheimer's. He wrote his memories into those notebooks so he wouldn't lose them. But..." she shrugged... "the notebooks are gone. This cigar box is all we have to solve the mystery. Are you in?"

I sighed. "We don't even know what's in there."

"Clues."

"You've peeked inside already?" I asked.

"This was strictly off limits. I know there will be something in here. There has to be. It's my mystery to solve. I'd like your help. I don't want to do this alone."

"We used to play Sherlock Holmes when we were kids."

"You were always Watson," she smiled.

"Only because you were so bossy."

"I won't tell you what to do this time," Alison said.

I tried to hesitate, to drag out the tension, but my curiosity was too strong. "I'm in."

Alison frowned. "Don't you want to know what we have to do?"

I shrugged. "You'll tell me."

She smiled again.

"When do we leave?" I asked.

"My parents are on their way. They should be here by tonight. We'll make plans in the morning."

"And they'll just let you go to who-knows-where with me?"

"Of course," Alison said. "I drink coffee now."

I honestly don't think I'll ever understand her.

Alison

"Is this supposed to help us?" Trey asked.

I wasn't sure either, but for the moment I just drank in the beauty of what Graypay had deemed worthy enough for his little cigar treasure box. Several pictures lay on top. First was a photo of Graypay and Grannie Stephie on their wedding day; Graypay had swept Grannie back in a graceful dip and was kissing her. I'd never seen this picture, but I recognized the dress Grannie Stephie was wearing from the picture on Graypay's dresser at home. Next was a photo of Eleanor, Henry, Graypay and Granny Stephie. They all looked ridiculously young and happy. The melody from my last dance with Henry drifted through my thoughts. How did Henry know that so much would change for me on this trip? And when would I feel all grown up? All I seemed capable of now was crying and sleeping. Then a terrible thought came to me: what if this wasn't the end of my change? What if there was something greater in the near future to carve me into an adult? Would it hurt? Would I still recognize myself? Was there any way to stop it?

Many other pictures were stacked together with worn edges as though Graypay had flipped through them every night before bed. Grannie holding my father right after he was born, before dad was crazed with deli schedules, rising bread and purchasing hocks of meat. There were pictures of Graypay, Grannie Stephie and my dad in front of Old Faithful, with friends in the Grand Tetons, standing below a Giant Redwood, and even on a Mississippi river boat. Other pictures were of buildings: a gas station, a church, an old farm. One was a group of children and a few adults in front of a white church with a steeple poking the sky. There was a nice looking couple standing on the top step of a store, Miller's Merchandise.

Below the pictures were newspaper clippings. Obituaries of Sue and Sam Elliott, Graypay's parents? He never talked about them. A long obituary for a man named John Miller, the man in the picture in front of the Miller Merchandise Store. The next obituary was for his wife, Betsy Miller. The last two newspaper clippings were obituaries for a Jacob and Ruth Paulson. They were listed together in one obituary, but had died almost a year apart.

Grannie Stephie's silver wedding ring etched with forget-me-nots sat on top of an envelope next to a gray stone. Inside the envelope was my birth announcement and a letter from my mother to Graypay asking him to come stay with us and help take care of me.

At the bottom of the box, tucked under everything, was a lock of black, silky hair tied in a yellow ribbon .

"What is this?" Trey picked up the hair.

I chuckled, "Seems a little obvious. It's hair."

"Why would he keep someone's hair?"

"Lots of reasons," I shrugged.

"Hey! Maybe it's that woman that we read about in the journal."

"I was afraid you'd say that."

He sat down next to me. "What?"

"I have to look for a woman. Not my Grandmother, but someone else that Graypay loved."

"And?"

"He was supposed to always be the perfect grandfather, not a man with a past."

"Everyone has a past." Trey put the lock of hair back in the cigar box and walked away.

Eddie

Stories. That's what the bible held. Summaries of what could really be great movies. Eddie consumed the New Testament from George in two days, reading it at every free moment between shifts. He craved more. Curiosity drove Eddie to the library where he quietly questioned a young man about where he could find more books on religion. The day ended with Eddie as the proud recipient of his first library card and a hardcover edition of the Bible, which Eddie could keep for three weeks.

The story of Creation – that would be an excellent flick with all they could do with computer generated graphics. Eddie tried not to think about Adam and Eve all naked in the beginning. That was the wrong way of thinking. Nudity was not bad when they were first in the Garden of Eden. Now it would be, so that movie would either never happen or involve strategic placements of plants and animals.

The simplicity of the stories frustrated Eddie. He longed to know more about Moses; the feelings Moses encountered when he continuously came into God's presence. When Joshua and the Isrealites attacked Jericho, Eddie had a difficult time visualizing all the details. His favorite movies had epic battle scenes where the characters true strength and courage were tested. That's what these stories needed.

And what did cities in ancient times look like? Were they as overcrowded as cities today? How did they manage all the waste? That's what Eddie wondered. He knew that his city was cluttered with roadside trash, but not human waste. That always puzzled him about those old cities. How did they manage all the little details of city life? What did it look like to not have plumbing? Not just on the months when the water bill wasn't paid, but always without running water. He knew that the city would probably be arranged differently, with the water well in the center or with a river flowing between the two sides of the city. Or, maybe the city would just be on one side of the river.

He wanted to know these things.

The people and the situations were much clearer when Eddie understood what they went home to, because that's what he had been taught. Well, not taught exactly. He'd caught that idea somewhere along the way.

In school, Eddie had trouble concentrating on the lessons instead of his aching stomach. Breakfast wasn't always served at one of his foster homes and he had to wait until lunch to eat at the school. The afternoon wasn't much better; his full stomach and the warmth of the room lulled him to sleep. Some teachers just let him sleep because it was easier than trying to teach him. Later that year there was a new teacher who obviously understood hunger. Mr. Moore. Eddie would never forget his name because Mr. Moore always had more of everything: more patience, stories, ideas, and more food.

One morning, Mr. Moore came outside before school started and asked if Eddie would like to help him prepare the classroom. Eddie didn't hesitate; it was cold outside and his coat was thin. It surprised him that teachers needed to prepare anything; wasn't the classroom always ready for the students? But Mr. Moore didn't really need Eddie's help. The day would have gone along just fine without clean chalkboards or a swept floor, but there was also food. On his desk, Mr. Moore had two steaming cups of hot tea, peanut butter and cucumber sandwiches, and two apples. After the boards were clean and the floor swept, there was still ten minutes before the bell rang. Mr. Moore invited Eddie to share his breakfast with him.

How different that day had been! With a full stomach of food he had earned, Eddie wasn't preoccupied with the groaning pain of his gut and was actually interested in the lesson on the colonies of early America. At lunch, Eddie ate again. Two full meals in less than four hours. He was still sleepy in the afternoon, but not exhausted. Just content. Mr. Moore told Eddie to come in early every morning because he could really use the extra help in the classroom, straightening books, cleaning the tops of desks, watering plants, sorting papers. Eddie agreed. For months he and Mr. Moore worked and ate breakfast together.

One afternoon Mr. Moore talked with the students about the American Revolution and how the English came to America expecting a quick victory, but found instead a long, difficult and bloody battle.

"Why do you think that happened?" he asked the class.

"The Americans had better weapons?" one student offered.

"On the contrary," Mr. Moore said. "The Americans had little more than old muskets. Some men fought with pitchforks. The Americans didn't have uniforms, proper lodging, or regular meals. Many of them lost their homes and families during the war and had nothing but what they wore and what they carried."

The students were appalled at the idea of owning only what you wore, but Eddie understood that. The last time a social worker came to take him to his new foster home, Eddie carried a trash bag holding the few clothes he owned.

"Was it because the Americans knew the land better?" a student asked.

"Perhaps in some instances," Mr. Moore agreed. "But what really made the difference, in my opinion, was the fact that the Americans were fighting for their own homes. They had to fight in order to live. They wanted fair representation, a stable government, and justice. They had very little to fight with, but they found what they needed in their courage, in their neighbors, and they stuck together." Mr. Moore looked directly at Eddie. "They had nothing but what they carried, and yet they won a war against the greatest nation of the time."

Eddie remembered what Mr. Moore had said to him for a long time. He didn't understand it, but he knew it was important. All these years later, that lesson came rushing back to his mind.

Eddie wasn't carrying a musket or doing battle, but he was in a fight for his life; an eternal battle of which he was now a foot soldier.

He skipped Deuteronomy after reading the first few chapters. He hoped that was ok, but it was all rules, not story. Eddie was coming to life from the power of the story and needed more, as if the words were food. The story of Jonah was good, he thought; how Jonah tried to ignore God, but was swallowed by a fish and delivered anyway. He read about David's appointment from God to become king, his son Solomon who was wise and was granted more wisdom from God. Samson's strength. But every one of those men failed.

How could that be? Eddie wondered. *How stupid were these men to hear God's voice, to know God had selected them for power, and then allow that power to corrupt them?*

Eddie's heart was heavy when he read that Moses never reached the land God had promised his people. It was most disappointing when Solomon turned evil and failed.

But Eddie had never heard God's voice. He wasn't royalty, he hadn't been chosen by a king or queen or even a CEO of anything. He was just a screw-up, a guy who grew up without parents, through the foster care system and had been on his own forever. What would God do with him? What good could Eddie possibly be? He was one of the bad guys. It was too late for him.

August 1954– April 1955
Jack Elliott

I took a job at the church as a maintenance man. The work suited me well after working outside for over two years. Grass and trees were my office furniture of choice; work boots and denim, my preferred attire. There was always something to fix, mostly shingles and doors, but I soon became adept at just about every repair needed, so much so that folks around town hired me to fix things around their homesteads. That's what kept us afloat during those winter months. I earned income in the form of eggs and fresh milk, patched clothes for Minnie, and spare change.

Minnie came with me many times to the church and to local houses and ranches for repair jobs. She learned quickly to tell the difference between a wrench and a Philips screwdriver. Mothers would sneak her little treats of biscuits or maple sugar candy into her pockets, and she played with other children.

Since Jacob was gone, there was no minister. The people still gathered on Sundays to read passages from the Bible and sing hymns. A new minister would be coming in a few months and that meant that Miss Ruthie, Minnie and I had to find a new place to live.

There were many things to pray about: a new place we could afford, a family for Minnie, the strength to let her go when we did finally find a family. I started praying for Miss Ruthie's health.

That winter was wickedly cold. For a few weeks, we couldn't leave the house with the winds howling like they were and the temperatures far below freezing. The cupboard was stocked with canned food, we brought the chickens into the back room, and I had built a wall of firewood just outside the backdoor. We managed, but it was a long, dark time. Miss Ruthie couldn't read the bible anymore. The tiny print made her eyes ache. During that cold spell, I read to her almost endlessly. She still tried to get up and cook, telling me it warmed her bones to be moving and near the woodstove. Just before the freeze broke, Miss Ruthie had taken up a comfortable chair right next to that woodstove. I even wrapped Minnie up with her, hoping that the joined body heat would help. She loved sitting there, cuddling with Minnie, but her teeth still chattered.

Four days before the new minister came, we buried Miss Ruthie. Mrs. Thomas and a few other ladies from town came and prepared Miss Ruthie for the funeral. We bundled up and walked her to the church. With no minister, the townsfolk all read passages from the bible and shared stories about her generosity, her fierce love for others, her little ways.

Minnie cried when Miss Ruthie was in the casket. She didn't understand. To be honest, I didn't either. How could a little thing like Minnie experience so much loss so young? When would it be enough? How would these losses figure into her emotions? Would I lose her too?

That was my greatest fear. I was a young man, twenty-two years old and responsible for this little life. I had no wife and no prospects for one. For the first time in my life, I didn't know what to do. I'd spent nearly seven years drifting around the country, leaving when I wanted to, living in places that would not be safe for Minnie.

I couldn't leave. I didn't want to leave her. There was no one here to take her. I knew that there had to be a family out there for her. In the back of my mind, I wondered if I was that family.

I had a few days after the funeral to clean out the house for the new minister, so I didn't spend much time worrying about it.

CHAPTER 15

Lies to a Police Officer

June 21ˢᵗ

Alison

Walking into the little room to view the lineup, my heart beat uncontrollably. What if the man wasn't here? What if he was still out there? And a scarier question, what if he *was* in the lineup? I would have to see his face again. Officer Decker came to the hospital just after lunch. That was an hour ago, giving me precious little time to prepare for this.

The little viewing room was slightly larger than a closet, with a large window on one wall. Through that window, I saw an empty room and a door.

"Are you ready?" the officer asked.

Ready? No.

But I didn't say that, not wanting to admit that I wasn't ready to see his face again. I nodded instead.

"Bring them in," the officer spoke into a microphone.

It was just his nose and his eyes that I remembered. His eyes were blue. His nose was very sharp; long and sharp. Maybe that would be enough of a memory to pull together other memories of the accident together and identify him.

He had climbed out of his SUV nearly unscathed and ran over to our car yelling, "Oh my God! Oh my God! I didn't see you!"

I remembered that. His voice. Scared and young. Rubbing my hand over my face, I tried to scrub off my anger. He didn't need to see us, just the stop sign. Why would it matter if we were there or not? He was supposed to stop!

But he didn't stop, couldn't stop. He should have stayed. He should have helped. Instead he ran. That was the crime.

The door on the other side of the window opened and a police officer lead in six young men. I looked down.

No. I was not ready to do this.

Daily Bread

Eddie

Was it too late for Eddie? That thought haunted him as he walked through his day. Was he really a bad guy? He'd never hurt anyone, never took anything from anyone who was bad off. Just little things. He only took little things. At first. When he left his last foster home, that's when he started stealing. He didn't steal for the fun of it. It had never been fun, always necessary. His last foster parents had been good people, but Eddie was too old for parents. They tried to get him to settle a bit and improve his grades in school, but he didn't care anymore.

The first thing he stole was bread. Just to make a sandwich. He had peanut butter, but no bread. He had beer too, but after spending money on the beer, he didn't have any left over for bread. He had known at the time that it was a dumb thing to do, but he had friends who wanted to come to his apartment to drink. As the evening ended, his friends went home to their parents' houses or to dorm rooms that offered three squares a day. Eddie didn't have that. Next door to the car wash was a little restaurant, but it cost him six dollars a day to eat lunch there. Two slices of bread was a small thing to take.

Stealing became easier the more he did it; like working out. It became a game after a while. When he had food, then he wanted more: a nice watch to keep up appearances of not being in need. A new coat. There was always the Salvation Army store or the charities that distributed used clothing. On occasion, Eddie had to go there. Winter was cold and he couldn't find a way to steal a coat. That was bigger and the chance of being caught was greater. Shoes were easier to steal. He just swapped out his old ones for the new. Take the tags off real subtle like and Bang! New shoes.

But food was always what he stole. It was nearly impossible to pay his rent and buy food on the little bit he made at the gas station. When he got the job a few years ago, the boss had a wife who baked cookies and bread and little dinners in plastic containers and would bring them to the station for her husband and Eddie. Never before had Eddie known a woman to be so giving and in love with her husband. He sure was glad she did. For those two years that she made that food, Eddie was rarely hungry. When she died, Eddie wept. Not only because he was going to miss her cooking, but because she really made Eddie's life better.

Her smile, the way she would light up that dingy gas station with her laughter and fresh baked bread. After her funeral, he tried really hard to not steal his food. But sadness was easier with the bottle of whiskey and that cost money. It was bread, again, that he stole first. Just bread. It was filling and smelled rich in the toaster. He didn't have any butter, but still enjoyed the crunch and the memory of a foster home long ago that smelled of freshly baked bread.

Now with his promise to never steal again no matter how hungry he was, he felt the weight of hunger throughout his body. A flitter of pride settled on his heart at that thought…followed quickly by a sense that he wouldn't last the winter.

No Doubt

Alison

Trey told me what he knew about police line-ups, admitting that everything he knew was from TV cop shows. I'm eager to tell him he knows nothing about line-ups. The men came out of a door and stood facing the window. OK, that part of Trey's line-up knowledge was correct. As the men walked into the room, I kept my eyes on my shoes. The moment would come to look up and have one of two results: the man who hit us would either be there or not. Having two choices seemed like it would be simple. It wasn't.

He was there. I recognized his face, the nervous look that lingered in the wrinkle between his eyes.

This man had hit us and left us. I knew that without any doubt. Yes, I had been injured and had only seen him for a moment, but I had also heard his voice. The officer had each man speak a line: "Oh my God, I didn't see you."

I knew it was him. What was the next step? Should I say, "That's him," and then go back to the hospital and wait for Graypay to wake up?

"What will happen to the man that hit us?" I asked the officer.

"He'll be charged with a hit and run. The time he would serve will depend on his past history; if he has a previous record or if this is a first time offense. Either way, this goes on his permanent record."

Permanent record. That seemed fitting. The damage to Graypay would be permanent. My trip across the country with my grandfather was certainly finished, ruined by this man's incompetence behind the wheel and made worse by his leaving us on the road. I tried to feel bad about pointing to the guilty man, that maybe if I was a little bit of a better person I would say he wasn't there and give the man a second chance.

Alzheimer's was permanent. No known cause and no known cure. Talk about a hit-and-run criminal.

"Do you see him, Miss Elliott?"

"I do." So much for a sweet teenager giving a guy a second chance. "Third one on the right."

"You're certain?"

"No doubt."

By the time Officer Decker drove me back to the hospital, my parents had arrived. It was a tearful greeting just outside Graypay's room. My mother asked me a dozen times if I was okay.

"Mom," I took her held her hand gently, "I'm fine. I'm bumped and bruised and sad, but I'm fine."

Wiping tears off her cheeks, she smiled and hugged me again before she turned on Trey. "Thank you!" She squeezed him tightly and cried on his shoulder. "You've taken such good care of Alison."

Trey was clearly uncomfortable. "I was driving," he said quietly.

My mother shook her head. "The accident wasn't your fault." She said it with full determination, but Trey seemed unconvinced.

Dad put his hand on Trey's shoulder. "It was a hit and run, son. The other man is to blame." Turning to me, "Speaking of that other man, how did the line-up go?"

180

I looked at Graypay's door. "I thought…well," I glanced at Trey, "I thought it would be different."

"Was he there?" Trey asked.

I nodded. "The officer wanted to know if we wanted to press charges. I said yes."

"Good." Trey's voice was on edge. He had been a rock of strength for me throughout this and I could see he was wearing thin; his face nearly transparent to the plague of emotions hiding within. It wasn't the accident or the concussion that was doing it. Glancing around the hallway, I didn't see Trey's parents. My dad told me later that because Trey was ok, they didn't see the point in coming. Apparently, my dad had a few choice words for his long-time friend, Trey's dad, but nothing seemed to make a difference.

I've always known how much my parents have done for me. They certainly worked long hours, but they are always there for me when I need them. Trey spent much of his childhood at our apartment. Graypay is as much his grandfather as mine. He had kept it all together while I was a blubbering puddle of tears. I wondered what I should do for him. A hug? My parents were standing right here. Being a coward, I just smiled at him awkwardly and told them about the man who had ended our trip. "He said he was sorry. Again. He had the nerve to ask me to not press charges."

"Really?" my mother asked.

"Yeah," I laughed bitterly. "I told him that I accepted his apology, but that his mistake wasn't just missing the stop sign. His crime was leaving. The officer submitted the paperwork for a court date. He said he would call as soon as he knew when. We can go if we want."

"We'll be there," my dad said.

"We might not be," I told him. "Graypay has a mystery for us to solve. Trey and I need to continue with this trip."

The look on my parent's face was new. Something Graypay had prepared me for, saying it was the result of parents realizing their child was an adult. Although I had been striving for this moment for years, my parents have been avoiding it.

"Be patient," Graypay had advised. "It's not easy for parents. They are growing up all over again with you and these growing pains are truly painful."

My mom, the forever calm one, asked for an explanation.

"Graypay's cigar box has clues for us to follow. With the journals stolen, they are the only clues we have to find her."

"Her?" dad asked.

"Someone Graypay used to know before Grannie Stephie. He wants us to find her." Repeating the story of my dream again, this time for my parents, I began to worry that my conversation with Graypay had been just a dream. But no, I held the box he told me to find and could see the evidence in the ribbon that there was someone waiting for me to find her. He didn't tell me the ribbon held a lock of hair, but I refused to doubt my conversation with Graypay.

Mom and Dad excused themselves and walked down the hall to discuss this new development. Trey and I watched as they kept their arms carefully crossed across their chests to hide any emotion as they debated whether or not they should allow their seventeen-year-old daughter to drive alone with a twenty-year-old college student into unknown lands of Montana and possibly Washington.

"I don't think they're going to go for this," Trey whispered.

"They will."

"Al, you're seventeen. You'd be just with me."

"Yes. You're my chaperone."

He shook his head. "Still."

"Trey, seventeen in my family means something. They just need time to talk it over."

"And you really think they will let us just drive away. In what? The car is wrecked. We aren't sure where we are going and we don't know how long it will take."

"I know. I've been thinking about that too. There will be a way." I looked at him and nudged him with my shoulder. "Trust me."

"Do your parents trust me?"

"To be a perfect gentleman as you chaperone me across the state lines to search for a woman my Grandfather used to know?" I looked at my parents again, still deep in discussion. "I trust you. That will count for something."

I was right. They talked for almost fifteen minutes in that hallway. When they came back they just said, "Okay." There were a few rules: we have to call in twice a day and stay in separate hotel rooms.

Trey seemed to turn into his father: his face was red and he was shaking his head.

"Are you okay?" Mom asked him.

"You are saying yes to two young people, a boy and a girl, to just drive away to who knows where. Wait! We don't even have a car."

Mr. Elliott smiled. "As luck would have it, someone already thought of that. Henry is on his way. He should be here by tomorrow night."

"And he's just going to let us take his car?" I asked.

Alison's mom laughed, "Well, that's why he's driving it here."

Trey ran his fingers through his hair. "Wait! If Henry was driving the car so we could continue our trip, then what was all that about?" he pointed down the hallway where my parents had stood in conversation. "Why go through that whole…charade…if you already knew that you would let us go?"

Mom smiled. "The plan was for Henry to go with you. He is the only one that knows all the details. Jack never told us exactly what was going on, but he did tell Henry. As we were making plans to come out, Henry told us you two would need a car. We asked him to go with you, but he believes that if he is with you, knowing everything, it will steer you away from Jack's intent."

I understood. "You mean he might unknowingly give us the answers we need."

"Making this whole thing easier," Trey added.

Mrs. Elliott looked at Alison, "That's why he didn't want to tell you about the Alzheimer's."

"Because knowing something to make it easy is bad?" Trey asked.

"According to Dad? Yes." Mr. Elliott scratched his chin. "Learning something on your own is far better. He believed that if Alison was just told that he was diagnosed with Alzheimer's, she wouldn't understand it as much. Discovering it on her own, finding the diagnosis herself…" he looked at me, "he wanted that to be a part of your adventure."

I could only nod. Even within the depths of his own illness, Graypay had thought of how to make me a better person, a more compassionate person.

Trey laughed. "Easy is bad. That's a new idea for me. Well, Alison, we have a cigar box of clues and tomorrow we will have a car. You were right."

"I know."

A Revelation

Trey

After being granted permission to continue on after Henry arrived, I slipped away from the Elliotts to give them time to be with Graypay. The neighborhood around the hospital was pretty nice and I wandered the sidewalks, drowning myself in pity, a very effective depressant, by the way.

My parents hadn't come.

The hospital called them the day of the accident to tell that I had been injured. When I woke up, the nurse told me that my parents knew what had happened and they would probably come soon. Hearing that, I felt strangely giddy. My parents were going to take time away from work to fly out here and be with me while I was in the hospital. The injuries on my list were limited to a bonked head and a few bruises, and I suddenly wished that my injuries were more severe out of fear that when they did arrive and saw me walking around, they would be angry that they had left all their responsibilities in Chicago to see me.

An hour later, mom called my hospital room to see how I was doing. "Fine, mom. Doc says I have a concussion."

"No broken bones?"

"Amazingly no," I said, feeling just that – amazing.

"And the concussion? Are you vomiting or having trouble with your vision?"

"Yes to the first and a little to the second."

I could hear mom passing along this information to my dad who responded with, "So it's not serious?"

"Trey, honey," mom continued talking to me, "how are Alison and Jack?"

At that point I didn't know how they were, although the nurse had told me that Alison would be up and around soon, but she was strangely cryptic about Jack. "I don't know, mom. I haven't left this room yet." Then I risked it all and just asked. "Are you coming?"

"To North Dakota?" my mom laughed. "Oh, heavens, I don't think so. If you are well enough to talk on the phone, it sounds like things are good. The nurse who called us told us that you would be able to leave by tomorrow morning."

Sure, I'm an adult and have been on my own at college for two years, but there was something churning in my stomach when my mother laughed at the idea of coming to the hospital to see me. Anger tightened around my tongue and I couldn't respond without giving away my feelings – and feelings were not something allowed with my parents. Duty was encouraged. A tough-it-up attitude was desired. Sticky emotions were strictly forbidden.

"Trey, dear, are you still there?"

"Yeah."

"We'll send you some flowers."

"Mom. Don't bother. If you want to send me something, send money. That seems more precious to you than anything else."

I hung up the phone. For the first time in my life, I had ended the conversation without letting my mom get the last word.

Immediately, the phone rang again. The nurse was still in the room and she raised her eyebrows at me when I didn't answer the phone. "Would you like me to just turn that ringer off?"

"Yes." I leaned back on my pillow and tried not to vomit again.

I'm sure if I had died in that car accident they would have cried the obligatory tears, but what in their life would be different? They never stopped working when I was born; in fact, they are proud of the fact that my mom actually held a meeting in the hospital room a few hours after I was born. The nurses took care of me during those four hours. Mom was rewarded for her heroic duty to her career with a raise and promotion and I was sent off to a daycare.

Seeing Alison with her parents, seeing how they trust her completely and are genuinely concerned with every decision she makes, really rubbed me wrong. They consider her ideas as true possibilities. My parents encouraged me to attend a university out of state, although dad was thoroughly involved in selecting my classes to steer me in the direction of medical school. Any suggestions of a different career had been met with laughter.

What do kids, whose parents don't love them, do? Let me rephrase. I know my parents love me but their love is a hard as a brick. They use those bricks to build my life - a tower of academic and financial successes and fill it with the latest of everything. I don't want a tower. I want a cardboard box that was a rocket ship yesterday, a puppet theater today, and will be a car tomorrow.

Can I sue them for emotional scarring? In this twisted world of law suits, I probably could, but what would that accomplish? It would only mark me as a cry-baby who is sad that his parents are dolts. If I can pick myself up, brush off the lint of their interference and do something great with my life, then that will be worthwhile. Science has always interested me, but that falls into the doctor-lawyer-physicist category that all parents dream of for their kids.

Artist. That would drive my dad nuts.

Writer. Even worse! He has no love for people who string together words to make up stories. Waste of time, he calls it, both for the writer and the reader. "Stick to what's real, son. That's where the money is."

Teacher. That's a possibility. Science teacher.

Mechanic. Ha! I could come to their holiday parties with grease under my fingernails and talk cars and carburetors' with dad's friends who have never looked under a hood let alone talked with me about anything other than what my future holds.

I could drop out of school altogether and just drift along, finding work as a cook or a general laborer. That doesn't appeal to me. For my own satisfaction, I really do want to finish school. Since the folks are paying, might as well make good use of that tuition money that keeps me out of their lives.

Banker. Businessman. Personal trainer. Physical Therapist. Restaurant manager.

The possibilities are endless.

After an hour or so, I headed back to the hospital feeling completely rejuvenated. In that quiet time I had come to two conclusions that would forever shape my life. One, my parents don't know how to love me, but that doesn't have to ruin me. Two, I was going to finish college seeking a degree of my own choosing. It was totally possible that dad would cut off my funding if I changed direction from his declared path, but that would be fine. I would get a job and put myself through school.

If Jack, at fourteen, can manage to start his life as an adult, then there was no reason why I, at age twenty, couldn't do the same.

I must have looked like a jolly speed-walker as I came up to the hospital doors, because Alison smiled when she saw me. "Well, you look better."

"I am."

She studied my face. "I expected you to be upset."

"Because my parents didn't come?"

She nodded.

"I was."

"But not now?"

"What would Graypay say? Life is far too precious to worry about what we can't change."

"Sounds about right."

I laughed. "You're looking at me funny. What's wrong?"

"You surprise me."

"You keep expecting me to act a certain way. But Al, I don't think I'm who you thought."

Her eyes twinkled. "I don't think you are the person *you* thought you were."

"I like the sound of that." And that was the truth.

CHAPTER 16

Great Changes Little Moments

June 22ⁿᵈ

Alison

Henry called when he was a few minutes away from the hospital. "My God," my dad said as he hung up the phone, "he must have driven all night."

I waited for him by the visitor's entrance and was delighted in that broken-heart way to see the pain on Henry's face as he nearly jogged to the door. Without a word he hugged me and we both cried. I honestly believed that at some point I would run out of tears, but I am obviously blessed with an endless supply of the buggers.

Henry kept his hands on my shoulders as he assessed my injury, which was now just a band-aid on my forehead and a slightly angry looking bruise around my eye. "You're ok." It wasn't a question. He was reading something within me that told him more about me than I understood myself.

"I am."

"And Jack?" he asked, almost grimacing at the expected answer.

"No change."

"But I see great changes in you," he winked. "You are finding what you need?"

"We have the cigar box. That's all that's left since the journals were stolen."

Henry thought about that for a moment before responding. "That will make things much more difficult, but I think if you start off in the right direction, you'll find what you're looking for."

I sighed. "Are you going to give me a hint?"

He smiled. "Let's go see your grandfather first. Then we'll discuss your plans and what you've learned so far."

Go West, Young Man

Trey

Alison, Henry and I ate together in the cafeteria, catching Henry up on what had happened so far. He was respectfully quiet as Alison and I took turns giving him every detail from the trip and explained what we had learned from the journals. I suspect that Henry didn't want to let slip a key piece of information that would help us, taking away from the struggle to find the answers ourselves.

"And where to you think you should begin your search?" he asked.

"Montana," said Alison. "That's where Graypay was headed when he left home. Maybe we'll find this church," she showed him the picture of a white-steeple church.

I sighed. "Talk about a needle in a hay-stack."

"No kidding," agreed Alison. "But we know that the railroad follows Highway 2. We know this is the direction he went."

"Good." Henry sipped on his tea.

"You mean, this is the right direction?" I asked.

"I mean that based on the information you have, this is a good choice."

Leaving the hospital and continuing this road trip without Graypay was harder than I expected. I was suddenly faced with a strange emotion. There isn't a name for what I felt and I wished there was because if I could know it, and name it, and then I could control it. With all the afternoons and weekends of my childhood spent with Graypay, I had come to trust him and love him like a grandfather. My maternal grandfather had died before I was born and my paternal grandfather was on the Board of Directors at the hospital where my father now worked and was just as crusty in his devotion to family as my father. Once again, I wished that I could be adopted into the Elliott family, to join the ranks of those who worked hard for every dollar and enjoy the comforts of homey apartments complete with hand-me-down furniture, mis-matched silverware and honest-to-God laughter.

I knew we had to leave, to find the mystery woman, to check off something on Alison's life list, but we were also leaving behind Jack, the man, the grandfather, the mastermind of imagination. He had plans for Alison and I on this trip that were now lost because he was lost. That was the clincher; a phase of my life was ending. When I left for college, I didn't look back. I was out of the house and free to decide for myself.

That past was now leaving me behind as I was now responsible for Alison and I want to do this right.

As we said our good-byes to Graypay and then Henry and the Elliotts, the laughter became quiet. We walked out of the hospital door and toward the parking ramp, knowing that we weren't just leaving behind a great man, but we were walking toward a completely different future. We were searching for someone we might not find - but my gut told me a treasury of discoveries awaited. There should have been a parade or something for us as we made our way out of the city and toward the highway; we left behind our former selves and drove directly into a mystery, complete with it's unknown 'bad guy'.

Heading toward Montana, Big Sky Country, we didn't speak much. Something huge had just happened and there was no fanfare for it. We had literally driven away from youth and directly into adulthood. How many people can say that they've done that?

Eddie

"What you usin'?" Stan asked.

"I'm not usin'." Eddie said.

"Well, you're on something, man. You smilin' like a damn fool."

"I suppose," Eddie smiled broadly.

"What's it called? This stuff?"

"I told you, man," Eddie shook his head, "I'm not on a drug and I'm not smoking anything."

Stan scratched the dark stubble in his cheeks. "That's what I thought. You don't smell like a drug. And you been gettin' to work on time all week, but you've been home late, so I figured you're usin'. But your eyes don't show it. So? What you been doin'?"

Eddie shrugged.

"Come on, Ed," Stan urged. "You're...happy. You didn't find something valuable in that chest, did you?"

Eddie nodded.

"Was it treasure like you thought? Were them notebooks from some celebrity or politician and you held them for ransom and they paid you cash and now you got extra money?"

Eddie laughed. It was part of his plan. Stan would never listen to Eddie talk about God or Jesus. It would turn him off. Stan was like that. If Stan saw someone else enjoying something, he wanted it. That's how Eddie and Stan both came to their downfall. Smoking their first cigarettes behind the school dumpster, feeling the heat of that first drag, muscles relaxing and mind sufficiently numbed. At the time, he thought his mind opened and he could think greater thoughts. Not true, he discovered too late.

Actually, it's lucky I realized that at all, what with my mind so boggled. Another miracle? Do miracles that small count?

Stan liked the feel of the nicotine, then moved on to pot and the occasional cocaine. He wasn't completely lost in the drugs, but enough so that he had lost a job or two over the years.

Stan pestered Eddie relentlessly over the next few days. "What are you doing after work? You look different, man. What is it? What's it called? Stop hoggin' it all!"

And because he said that, Eddie didn't want to tell Stan that he was high on God. Trippin' on religion. Jazzin' for Jesus. Eddie just wouldn't risk losing his friendship over this new way of thinking he found.

"Ah, but dear," one of the old church ladies, Dorothy, patted Eddie's arm when he mentioned his concern, "that's exactly the point. God is asking us *all* to be brave. He wants us to share His Good News. That's why Jesus came."

"Yeah, and look what they did to him," mumbled Rosie, a practical ol' gal who still wore lace over her head inside the church.

"Precisely my point," Dorothy clapped her hands together. "It's not about this life, but the next."

Eddie knew she was right, knew that he should, but felt afraid.

"So you'll talk to your friend?"

"I'll try. Next time he asks."

"Good." Dorothy patted Eddie on the arm. "Very good."

Stan usually came by after work. Five-thirty. Eddie was ready. He had food too, courtesy of The Pantry. Stan would likely stay longer if there was food.

Five forty-five.

Six o'clock.

Eddie had the bible out and open. Perfect place to start. Jack's journal chest was on the TV tray too. That's where it all started for Eddie. Maybe if Stan would read Jack's story, he would be pulled to Jesus and then he could read the bible.

Could Stan even read?

He's seen him look at the newspaper, but if Eddie asked about an article, Stan would just shrug and toss the paper at him and say, "It's all right there. Read it yourself."

Six fifteen.

No Stan.

At six twenty-four, Eddie's door rattled on its hinges. He had been reading the book of Revelation when the angel hurled the gold censer down to the earth causing thunder, lightning and earthquakes. For a moment, Eddie thought it had actually happened and his apartment would come tumbling down.

Lou barged into the apartment. "Ed, man, let's go. Now. Gotta go now!" He pulled Eddie's arm and lifted him right out the door.

"What?" Eddie stopped Lou's tugging.

"Stan ... Stan was crossing Alpine and some truck came. I don't know who didn't see who, but Stan got hit."

"You were there?"

"Not right away. Stan usually crosses around there and I was lookin for the money he owes me. I saw him though. Then ambulance drivers told me they's taking him to St. Mary's. It's closest." Eddie sat back down, his knees suddenly too weak to hold him up. He reached for Jack's notebook and his bible, hugging them close to his chest. "What are you doing?" Lou grabbed Eddie's arm. "Ain't you gonna go see him?"

"Yes," Eddie stood. "Yes. Right now. There still might be time."

They ran all the way to St. Mary's. Twelve blocks. St. Mary's stood on St. Johns' Avenue like a white stone monument.

The information desk attendee directed them to the emergency room. The nurse there directed them to bed six. "Before you go in," she said, "your friend has been hurt badly. The doctors have stopped the bleeding, but…" she shook her head. "It's too soon to know." She had anticipated Eddie's question. "You may see him for a few minutes."

Running here, Eddie hoped he wouldn't be too late. That if Stan was going to live, he hear God's Word. But now? Now Eddie didn't know if Stan could hear him.

Why didn't I tell him yesterday when he asked?

Lou and Eddie stared at the bed. How could that be Stan? Blankets, bandages, wires and machines surrounded the body like a web.

Eddie swallowed his fear and stood close to Stan, trying not to gag on the ripe stench of blood. "Stan?"

Stan opened his left eye just a bit.

"Stan. It's Eddie. Can you hear me?"

Stan didn't move anything except his eye. "You asked me what it was that was making me so happy. I'm gonna tell you and you gotta listen close." Stan closed and opened his eye. "Good. Good," Eddie steeled himself. "Stan, now don't you laugh, but them journals I stole, those notebooks in that wooden chest? Remember? Well, I read them. The man who wrote in those notebooks lived a life like we did, you know, with parents like ours, but he did it different. He followed a

199

different set of rules. I'm tryin' to do that now. I see my life different. Better.

"The man that wrote those journals talked about a great book that could save lives. It can heal people and make people feel different, better about life." Eddie held up the bible from George. "The Bible. I've read in here that you can only get to heaven if you believe in Jesus. Jesus came here to earth and gave us a bunch of stories that tell how to live better. People didn't believe him and other people plotted against him and had him executed. They killed him, Stan, and all he wanted to do was to bring us closer to God.

"Now you listen to me, Stan! Jesus wasn't done. They killed him but he took that and turned it on its head. Jesus died so he could defeat death. Through our trust in Jesus, he can do the same for us.

"I've given my life to God. I'm still figurin' out what that means, but I'm not scared of stuff like I was. Like death. He defeated death, Stan! Think about that. Those men had him killed, but he came back to life! He can heal you too, Stan. Do you believe?"

Stan blinked.

"That has to mean yes," Eddie laughed. "Good, Stan, good! Now I'll speak these words and you repeat them in your head."

Eddie thought his heart would pump its way right into his brain. He had no idea what the words were, but he also had the feeling that he didn't need to worry. God was there with him and Eddie felt Jesus standing at the foot of the bed. "Heavenly Father, please forgive me for all the bad things I've done. I know I was wrong. I know only you can forgive me. Forgive me, Father."

A tear rolled from Stan's eye into his ear. "Good, good!" Eddie cried. He turned to the nurse. "I need a cup of water."

She hurried from the room and returned in less than a minute with a white Styrofoam cup. Eddie quickly took off the lid and the straw and leaned over Stan again. "I'd like to baptize you."

Stan blinked.

Eddie had no idea how to baptize anyone and he wasn't even sure if anyone except a priest or minister could, but he also knew that God would understand his intention. "Lord, I ask You to bless this water. I bring my friend Stan into Your light and love." He dipped his thumb into the cup of water and made the sign of the cross on Stan's forehead. Years ago, Eddie had seen a baptism and the priest poured water over the baby's head three times. Eddie dipped his thumb into the water and made the sign of the cross a second and third time. "In the name of the Father, and of the Son, and of the Holy Spirit. Amen."

A wave of relief settled on Eddie. He had made it. Stan had heard Eddie's words, God's Joy, and hopefully, agreed to the baptism. A twinge of fear prickled Eddie's chest as he wondered whether Stan's blinking meant Yes or No. Yes. They were Yes! This was not the time to second guess.

The nurse escorted Eddie and Lou to the waiting room when the doctor came into the cubicle. After his surgery, hours later, a different nurse came to get them. The doctor waited for them outside the curtain wall of the Intensive Care Unit.

"Your friend sustained a lot of injuries. He had a very low platelet count which resulted in a vast amount of blood loss. During surgery, I was able to re-inflate his lung and mend a few other areas..." he hesitated. "I'll not try to deceive you. I don't think your friend will make it. His breathing is weakened from years of smoking and his liver is damaged from alcohol."

Eddie took a deep breath and nodded.

"You are welcome to stay with him until…" he didn't finish, but Eddie knew he was going to say *until he dies.*

"Amy, the nurse who brought you to him earlier, told me that you baptized him."

Eddie held his bible closer. *Is this doc going to tell me I can't do that?*

"If you would like to read to him," the doctor pointed to the bible Eddie held, "I think that would be a good thing."

A nurse came in with two chairs. The doctor returned a few minutes later with coffee and donuts for Eddie and Lou. Eddie looked at the little Bible and prayed, "Lord, guide me to the words that Stan needs to hear." He let the Bible fall open and he laughed when he saw where God had led him.

"What?" Lou asked.

Eddie turned to his friend. "If God speaks to you, will you listen?"

Lou stared at him. Eddie didn't know what was going through his mind, but Lou didn't laugh, didn't blink, and he didn't walk away.

Eddie wiped his eyes and turned to the Bible. "The Gospel according to John. Chapter one. In the Beginning was the Word, and the Word was with God and the Word was God."

May 1956
Jack Elliott

Other than letters and postcards to the Miller's, I had not set foot in Ohio since I left. My heart pulverized my chest as I realized I hadn't missed home. I loved my parents but I never liked them. I was born to travel – or so I thought. Now I felt I had been born to care for Minnie.

This time I purchased a sleeping car on the train and packed more clothing than ever. Minnie's clothes were small, but I took everything we owned. I sent a telegram to Mr. and Mrs. Howard to tell then I was coming. I didn't tell them about Minnie. Many reasons for that: the cost for each word in a telegram and what would I write? *I will be bringing home a four-year-old Chinese girl for whom I responsible? No one in Montana would take her because she looks different, but I love her and want her.* I would just explain things when I got home and they would understand.

Before we left, I sent another round of letters to Jacob's friends, telling of Miss Ruthie's death and my plans to go to Ohio. I included the Howard's address should someone know of a family in the Midwest.

I had also been in contact with a lawyer to legally become Minnie's guardian. This had been Jacob's plan too, but after his death, Miss Ruthie asked me to pray about it. I wished God could speak to me the way he did to Samuel – to tell me if this is part of His plan for Minnie. For me.

203

As I reflected in prayer, I understood that God had *shown* me. Minnie runs to meet me in the yard every time I come home. She falls asleep on my shoulder every night. She kisses my cheek in the morning when she wakes up before me, which happens more often than not.

A fraction of me did not want this responsibility. Something like this was never in my plans. Never. I knew of no other man my age and unmarried and responsible for a child. It felt strange to think that I was taking her home – to my childhood town, to the place from where I had run.

People in Montana were used to seeing Minnie and I together: a blond-haired man and a three-year old Chinese girl. They knew her story and accepted me as her guardian. That changed on the train. My guardian papers were tucked away in my shirt pocket with a third of my money. We left in the evening and settled into a sleeper car. They next morning in the dining car, we turned heads. Under the scrutiny of passenger's eyes, I tried to ignore the blazing stares and the whispers. One dining car attendee was bold enough to ask if I would be bringing any food back to the car for my wife.

That's all they saw in us: an unmarried man with a foreign child. It didn't worry me then – or ever. These people hadn't been to our town and they didn't know Minnie. She sat on her knees in the chair next to me because she was a "big girl" and wanted to look out the window. She ate a muffin and drank tea with milk.

"Jack-Jack. I see fly-bees." Her little voice delighted my soul. I leaned over the table and looked to see the fly-bees – geese. "Where are the fly-bees going?"

"Home," I said. "All we have to do is follow the fly-bees home."

I didn't trouble myself with the others on the train. Jacob had told me long ago that anger only hurts the person who feels it. Their thoughts were nothing to me. I sat back and enjoyed watching the fly-bees race the train.

There is Nothing I Lack

Eddie

Stan died as Eddie was reading from the Gospel of Matthew. He wasn't reading straight through the Gospels, but was skipping around, just reading the parables. Eddie thought Stan would like those the best. In the past, when someone died, Eddie knew that it was the end for that person. Anyone Eddie had known was certainly in Hell; except for one foster mother. She had to be a Saint. Stan's death didn't have that same feeling. There was a shift in the room a moment before the heart monitor's beep became one, long tone. It felt as if someone else had walked into the room; opened a door and let a breeze through. A breeze that didn't move the curtains but did raise goose bumps on his skin. Even Lou felt it. They looked at each other, then Stan. The body in the bed was no longer Stan.

"He's gone," Eddie sighed.

Lou sniffed. "You think he's – you know – you think he's alright?"

"Yeah, man. He's all good." Eddie turned back to the bible and continued to read as the nurses came in and cared for Stan's body. They did it quietly. Reverently. Eddie turned to the Book of Psalms and read the 23rd Psalm. He had heard it plenty of times in movies, but today the words made sense.

Before Jack's journals, Eddie was always hungry for food, desiring more clothes, new shoes, the latest stuff. He had cheated and lied to surround himself with things. Strangely, through his sin, in the act of stealing Jack's chest, Eddie had discovered the green pastures and was restored. The right path was one of joy: joy of having a meal that he had actually paid for, happiness found in charity, the cleansing zeal of faith. Sure, Eddie had walked through a dark valley his entire life. His childhood was nothing but foster home after foster home, leaving him with the knowledge that no one loved him and no one cared. If he was going to do anything with his life, it was up to him to take it.

Just a few weeks ago, 'taking it' meant literally that. If you see it and want it, take it. Now he had taken something new. Or had something new taken him? He took the first step toward a new life when he read the journals. Step two when he prayed in the grocery store. Step three in finding refuge in the church. He had taken those actions, and God had been there all along, planting Jack's journals in a beautiful chest, having George the New Testament Man outside the grocery store, the little, sweet ladies at church. Every time Eddie had taken a step on the right path, he saw that God was already there waiting for him.

Eddie knew that death was no longer a threat to him. God promised eternal life in heaven. That was hard to believe. It boggled his brain to think that anything could last forever. Things of this world never do. That was the difference. This world is a world of things. Of bodies. Of desires. Eternal life in heaven is without a physical body, without possessions. Why wouldn't a soul last forever? What is in a soul that can die?

Psalm 23

> *The LORD is my shepherd;*
> *there is nothing I lack.*
> *In green pastures you let me graze;*
> *to safe waters you lead me;*
> *you restore my strength.*

You guide me along the right path
for the sake of your name.
Even when I walk through a dark valley,
I fear no harm for you are at my side;
your rod and staff give me courage.
You set a table before me as my enemies watch;
You anoint my head with oil;
my cup overflows.
Only goodness and love will pursue me
all the days of my life;
I will dwell in the house of the LORD
for years to come.

-New American Bible

May 1956
Jack Elliott

The second night on the train, sleeper cars were full. I spent a very uncomfortable night sleeping on benches of the passenger train car. Minnie slept well, mainly because she had room to spare on the bench when she stretched out. In North Dakota we had a few hours before the train completed the switching of cars and cargo, so we went in search of a grassy area to play. A field just outside of town was perfect. An open grassy area thick with wild flowers for Minnie to pick surrounded by trees on three sides and the backs of stores on main street on the fourth side. Minnie looked puzzled.

"What's troubling you?" I asked.

"Stars aren't out yet."

"You're right. We'll do star stories on the train tonight and see if we can catch up with them. Right now, I need to take a nap. Let's both take a snooze so we can stay up late tonight for star stories." Minnie looked less than thrilled, but eventually she did lie down in the grass, using my arm as a pillow. I sighed in relief that she was cooperating so well. What felt like moments later, a shadow blocked the sun, waking me.

"No sleeping here, son," the policeman said.

"Sorry." I said sitting up. "We didn't sleep well on the train."

"Who's we?"

I looked to where Minnie had curled up. She wasn't there. "Minnie!" I stood and scanned the clearing for her. "Minnie! Where are you?"

"Who?" the officer asked again.

"My Minnie," I choked back panic. "She's my... she's mine. I take care of her."

"Alright, son," the officer said. "Let's calm down and I'll help you."

Calming down was impossible. Muscles in my body that I didn't know existed clenched and fluttered in fear. I didn't know where she was. Minnie was my responsibility and I had lost her. Being a parent, a guardian, was the most important thing to me and here I was failing at it.

Officer Phillips took a description of Minnie and sent out his two deputies to scour the woods and houses around town for her while he and I went from store to store, asking if anyone had seen a little Chinese girl wearing a blue dress and possibly carrying flowers.

Twenty minutes after we began our search, I heard her tiny voice call, "Jack-Jack! Come have tea."

Just across the street, several little girls had openly welcomed Minnie to their tea party, complete with invisible tea and real cookies.

Running across the street, I reached Minnie in record time and scooped her into my arms and cried freely on her boney shoulder. "I didn't know where you were. Minnie, you scared me to death!" Minnie cried too, not out of fear at having been lost, but because I was crying. "Don't ever leave me like that again, Minnie. Please always stay near me."

She touched my wet cheeks and promised.

Officer Phillips checked the paperwork that Miss Ruthie had made with the lawyer proving that I was in fact a legal guardian for Minnie. I bought a few sandwiches and apples at the mercantile, and Officer Phillips graciously drove us back to the train station where I upgraded our tickets to a sleeper car.

CHAPTER 17

Dr. Ben and the Answer

June 23rd
Eddie

After Stan was taken from the room, Eddie went to the church. He sat there for hours, staring at the crucifix above the altar.

What was in a soul that could die?

The only thing Eddie knew that was truly perishable was sin. Sin kills. Sin destroys. With God, sin dies. A soul that is going to be welcomed into heaven must not have sin.

"Lord forgive me. Forgive me of all my mistakes, all the things I done wrong. Take away my evil side and give me a good side. I want to be like Jack, like Paul who was blind until he followed Your ways. Lord, forgive me."

"Eddie?" a man's voice called his name.

Eddie looked at the crucifix in awe. Had the Lord just called his name?

"Are you Eddie?"

Turning around, Eddie saw the doctor who had helped Stan. Eddie felt foolish but didn't let it show. "I'm Eddie. I remember you, Dr. Lawrence.

"It's Ben. I'm only Dr. Lawrence when I wear the scrubs. May I join you?"

Eddie slid over in the pew a bit and Ben sat down. "You did a good thing today."

"Stan was a good guy. A little lost, maybe, and prone to addictions and borrow money too often, but a good guy."

"Eddie, you seem like a man of great faith."

Eddie chuckled. "That's a first."

"If I may be honest, it does seem like you have a story to tell."

"I sure do. Doesn't matter now. I've made a choice to let the past be the past and to start on a new journey into a better future."

"That's a difficult thing to do."

"But it had to be done. It was almost … well, I think God took one of my sins and turned it on its head, bringing me here. I never knew that could happen."

"God did the same thing for me," Ben confessed.

"You? But you're a doctor."

Ben smiled, "Yes, but I'm human first. For years I thought I knew what I wanted, and what I wanted was to make my own rules. You know the saying, if it feels good and doesn't hurt anyone why not do it? Learned pretty quick that that idea is the dumbest way to live. So many of my friends at the time wanted the freedom to live in a way they were never allowed to under the thumb of their parents. But it wasn't a thumb that pressed us down. If we had any sense at all, we would have realized it was guidance." Ben laughed. "Now I find myself doing the same thing to my own children."

Eddie nodded. He had no family, but imagined that if he did have kids, he would keep them on the straight and narrow path so they didn't make the same mistakes.

"I talked with the hospital deacon about you," Ben said. "We have an idea. I'd like to offer you a job. Well, it's kind of a job. We can't pay you in money, but I can get you a pass to the cafeteria. There are many patients with no family or friends to visit. Even those who do have loved ones spend hours alone while the world outside the hospital walls goes on. If you could come and read to them, talk and pray with these people, the hospital will pay you in meals."

How about that? Eddie thought. *That would ease the pinch of buying food. Then I would have enough money from working at the gas station to pay for my rent each month and save a little.* "Thank you."

"And this," Ben handed Eddie a box. Inside was a bible. Old and New Testaments. "I heard the words you used with your friend, the prayers you spoke. You're Catholic. Then I saw you here and I knew that this was meant for you. It's a Catholic bible. Extra stories. I know you'll like it."

May 1956 – June 1957
Jack Elliott

My letter arrived two days before Minnie and I did. Mr. and Mrs. Howard met me at the train station and stared open-mouthed when I stepped off the train with Minnie in my arms. Mrs. Howard immediately started to cry, whimpering about all how all her prayers that I would be a 'smart boy' had fallen on deaf ears. The stern look on Mr. Howard's face raised icy sweat down my back.

"Jack," he said. "Who is this?"

I cleared my throat. "Mrs. Howard, Sir, this is Minnie. She's my charge. I'm her guardian."

Wiping her nose with a kerchief, Mrs. Howard looked up at me. "She's not yours?"

"No, ma'am." I gave them the abbreviated version of Minnie's story, which brought more tears to Mrs. Howard's eyes and a smile of pride to Mr. Howard.

"We are right proud of you, son. Come on, let's get the two of you fed." We didn't go to their house, but to the store where I had spent so many hours working for the money to start my adventure out west; an adventure that began with running away from one family and discovering another. We drove past the road that would have taken me to my folks place, but I knew that I would not find anything there. While I was a Ranger in Wyoming, Mrs. Howard wrote to tell me that Ma had died during the winter and Pa followed a month later. I was an orphan. I was caring for another orphan. I didn't know what the future would hold for Minnie and I, but I knew that I would do anything for her. I just didn't know that doing what was best for Minnie would slice a giant hole in my soul.

Life with the Millers settled into a comfortable routine quickly. Minnie immediately loved Mrs. Miller but was slow to like Mr. Miller only because of his size. With his patient nature, in less than a week, Minnie was hugging him goodnight without any form of bribery on my part.

During the day, we all worked in the store, including Minnie. The older ladies in town loved to ask Minnie to save their aching backs and reach for things that were on the bottom shelves. The town fell in love with her constant smile and unending energy as quickly as I had. Every day when the mail came, I secretly prayed that there would be no letter from her family. They were terribly selfish prayers, for sure. What family, no matter how extended, wouldn't want to know of the whereabouts and welfare of one of their own? And yet, she had been with Ruthie and then me for almost a year.

As the weeks slid into the last days of summer, Mrs. Miller took Minnie to the elementary school to enroll her. She could already read and do some simple math computations, all courtesy of Mr. Miller, so the principal had Minnie enrolled in first grade instead of kindergarten. Running into the store, Minnie jumped into my arms to tell me all about her first day of school, her teacher and the students. "Oh! I found this," she reached into the pocket of her dress and handed me a lumpy stone. "It's just for you, Jack-Jack!" Running off again, she headed out the back door to swing on the old tire Mr. Miller put up for Minnie and her friends to play on after school.

"I love the little things from her," I commented as I pocketed the rock.

Mr. Miller agreed. "I have a box upstairs with all the little pebbles and seed pods our daughter thought I would like. To someone else it would seem a collection of junk. Not to me though."

"Did you look carefully at that stone, Jack?" Mrs. Miller asked as she tied her apron on.

"No. Why?"

"Look again. That's no simple stone."

Examining it further, I couldn't see what Mr. Miller was talking about. "Ok. I give. What's the big deal?"

Walking to me, she took the stone and turned it, then held it up for me to see from a specific point-of-view.

"It's a heart," I realized.

"That little thing just gave you a heart of stone," Mrs. Miller laughed. "Something you will most likely need if her family ever writes."

She was right about that. Two weeks later, the letter arrived. It was from Pastor Edward, the man who replaced Jacob.

Dear Jack,

I do hope this letter finds you and Minnie is excellent health and good spirits. As you requested, I am writing to you with information about Minnie's family. They arrived from China. A group of about fourteen have come here looking for family. One of them speaks fairly good English and from her I have been able to discern that Minnie's family came here in order to prepare a place for the rest of the family. After Mr. Thomas at the General Store explained that they had died in a fire, they assumed the little girl had too. It was only a few weeks later when one of them saw a picture of you and Minnie that Mrs. Thomas had up in the store that they realized that there was a survivor. Like I said, their English is fairly good, but not good enough that they understood that the little girl had lived. It was especially difficult because no one here ever knew her real name. Her name is Mayfang, by the way. I'm certain I am spelling it wrong, but that is how it sounds.

They have asked me to write to you to bring Minnie back here. Her family is anxiously awaiting your arrival.

Sincerely,
Pastor Edward

CHAPTER 18

Museums of Inspiration

June 24th

Alison

After driving all day yesterday, and four hours today, we stopped at the first interesting place we saw. Stopping was a no brainer. The plains of Eastern Montana are amazingly unpopulated. There wasn't much to look at, but the view was far from simple. As we drove, those crumpled hills seemed to shift as though a giant lay just beneath the surface of grassy blankets and was slowly rousing to the sunlight. One of the treasures hidden by the hills was a museum. At first glance, the expansive gravel parking lot bordered a building that had been added onto over the years, each time with a different architectural design. Trey didn't ask if I wanted to stop, he just pulled into the lot and parked.

"I need a break."

"I'm sorry I can't help you drive," I said. Henry's car had a manual transmission, a skill I had not yet acquired.

"I don't mind driving, as long as we can stop now and then."

Truth was that I wanted to stop, too. "Interesting place."

"A museum, I think," Trey guessed, "or a really elaborate gift shop."

Turned out to be both. For a few dollars we could tour the entire place and then purchase trinkets in the gift shop. There was even a restaurant of sorts: a freezer with microwavable dinners and a microwave. We ate first then decided to tour a little of the museum.

It wasn't arranged like any museum in Chicago. Instead of priceless items behind glass or sophisticated miniatures depicting moments form history, this was a collage of items spread out on tables and book shelves. Signs were posted everywhere to please not to touch the displays - a sample of trust I've never seen before.

Rag dolls were propped against boxes that stood on end so the interior of the box faced outward displaying trinkets, tools and framed photographs. The more I wandered it became clear that each room was not about a specific time period of Montana's history, but a particular theme.

As we ventured further through the maze of displays, I was thrilled to find an entire room for toys: wooden toys crafted by skilled fathers for their children, tin toys purchased through the Sears and Roebuck Catalogue which was neatly lying on a pedestal for museum-goers to flip through. Trey spent most of his time in the agricultural room, packed with actual farming equipment as well as photos of farmers, their families, information on the crops and recipe books written by the hands of frontier-women who used every source of food possible to create, what appeared to be, delicious meals for families.

"Look at this," Trey pointed to a book titled *Country Living*. "They actually have a section in here on how to prepare people for burial."

"Seriously?" I asked, suddenly intrigued.

"Amazing," Trey said, standing straighter and looking around the room.

"You really like this stuff."

"Yeah, it's interesting. All the people who lived out here before it was a state and even after, they were…" he hesitated, "…brave. I think that Graypay was right, people now-a-days are softer when it comes to really living."

"I think many people would be offended by that," I said.

"I was when Graypay said it. Now looking at this room and this whole place, I agree. People lived and built their homes, grew their food, traded, went to church, and … lived. It looks incredibly difficult and satisfying."

"You think you might like a life like this?" I asked.

He looked around at all the tools, the display of homespun clothing, the photographs of pumpkins the size of a small cars. "I think this life is no longer possible. But, yeah, if I could find a way to simplify my life, to find a little plot of land and be self-sufficient, that would make me very happy."

"I almost hate to ask, but what about your parents?"

"They would hate it," he smiled, that old twinge of mischief sparkled in his eyes. "But I wouldn't choose this because it would drive them crazy. I honestly think I would love living in the country. Have a house away from the city, a garden and some animals. A little office in town to see patients…" he stopped and looked at me in surprise.

"You just said you wanted to see patients!" I whispered.

Trey's eyes were wide and he looked a little pale. "I *did* say that! Do I want that?" He looked to me for an answer.

"Do you need to know today?"

His shoulders relaxed and he laughed at himself. "I guess not. Although," he sighed, "I think I'm thinking more clearly than I have in a long time." He hesitated for a moment, then asked, "And you? You haven't been writing in your journal as much. No poetry."

I shrugged. "I know there is a poem within me about all this, but it won't come out of my pen. That sounds strange, I know, but that's what it feels like." That's all I could say. Like my pen that wouldn't write the correct words, my mouth couldn't say all the things it wanted to. The trauma of the last few days stirred up such strong words and emotions in my heart that my brain couldn't decipher them all. I managed to keep a list of phrases that maybe someday, I could craft into a poem. For now they are just scraps of thoughts, pieces of a bigger picture that I can't see. Not yet, anyway.

I tried to enjoy the agriculture room as much as Trey, but I just didn't find it quite as inspiring as he did. The next room, however, nearly socked the breath right out of me. The room was just as large as the previous room, but was partitioned by bookshelves. The second section I wandered through held mostly pictures, all neatly framed. In the center of it all was an old church pew. I strolled along the black and white photographs of various churches throughout the state. Tall white steeples gleamed, people stood stoically for the cameraman, priests and pastors stood holding their bibles.

And there it was plain-as-day: a photograph of that white church, the same one Graypay had in his cigar box. Handwritten in the lower corner was a date: 1945.

"Trey," I called his name, but my voice was barely a squeak. "Trey!" I shouted, overcompensating.

He ran into the room. "Are you okay?"

"Look," I held the photograph out for him.

"Is that the same one?" he asked.

I nodded.

He smiled. "I think we need to search for more clues, Sherlock."

"Quite right," I answered in my best British accent. "I wonder where this is? Do you suppose the lady at the front desk would know?"

"I doubt it. This state is huge. There's no way she would be able to recognize some church from 1945." He looked around. "I have an idea." Flipping the frame over, he slid the back off and took the picture out of the frame.

"Can you do that?" I asked, feeling very criminal-like with the "Don't Touch the Displays" sign posted right above the shelf.

"I think the question you should be asking is, should we? Probably not, but…" he handed me the photo. "Chinook. Where's that?"

"No idea," I admitted. "But the gift shop has maps. I think we just found our next clue."

That wasn't all we found. As Trey put the photo back in the frame, I found another. I took down a picture from the shelf and stared at a familiar face. Standing between two older men was a very young Jack Elliott.

Trey looked over my shoulder. "I don't believe it."

"Look at that," I pointed to the building behind the three of them: General Store. "This must be where he lived."

"He never told you where he lived?"

"He called it the 'Town of Many Memories' sometimes. No, I don't think he ever told me. Or if he did, I don't remember."

"This place looks really small."

225

"That I do remember. A man was in Montana surveying for the railroad in the late 1800's or early 1900's, I don't remember which. He saw that land and filed a claim on it. The town almost wasn't even a town except for a little building that the store was in and an inn, which served more as a communal living building. Around the time Graypay lived there, a few more buildings popped up, but it sounded like it was destined to be a forever small place or a ghost town."

Trey slipped the photo out of the frame, but the back was blank. "That's incredibly unhelpful. Remind me when we get back to Chicago to write the date and location on the back of every picture."

"You'll have to print them all out first," I teased.

"Right." Trey looked around. "Let's take this to the front desk. Maybe she'll know how we can find out where this is."

Joan, the front desk attendant, was thrilled to have a task outside of dusting the endless shelves of trinkets. "Let's see," she poised her spectacle on the end of her nose and peered at the photo. She took it out of the frame to check the back. Trey didn't tell her that there was nothing written on the back out of fear that she would refuse to help them if she learned that they had already examined it without permission. "Hmmm," she muttered, "very unhelpful."

"I agree," Trey said.

"Folks back then didn't always think to write on the back of every picture. Probably thought these photographs would always stay within the family or at the church," Joan explained. "But time strolls along and carries little pieces of our lives with it. Documents and photographs are scattered all over the country."

"What about this picture?" I handed her the one with Graypay in front of the General Store.

"Hmm…" she took it and examined it closely. "Let's see," she muttered to herself as she rummaged in a drawer and pulled out a thick magnifying glass. For several moments, she hunched over the photograph and finally sat up, smiling. "Look." She handed me the magnifying glass and pointed to a truck parked in the background. I leaned over and peered through the glass.

"Is there a sign on the door?" I asked.

"Yes. McKleary Meats."

"Does that help us?" Trey asked.

"It might," Joan smiled. "Wait here." She left us standing in the front room of the museum for almost ten minutes. She returned lugging a massive book. "Our answer might be in here."

"What is that?" I asked.

"This was the project of one of the secretaries over in Helena. She documented businesses, their products, what they manufactured, their annual income, their donations, and their delivery routes."

"But they probably delivered all over Montana and maybe into North Dakota," Trey said.

"Probably." Joan answered, ignoring Trey's pessimism as she scoured the pages for McKleary Meats. Trey picked up the magnifying glass and continued to examine a photograph.

"You're right," Joan said. "McKleary delivered on routes all along highway 2, and down into Billings and Helena and just about everywhere in between." She sat back disappointed.

"One of those cities begin with 'Ga'?" Trey asked.

"What did you find?" Joan leaned over to look at the photograph Trey had.

"This church has a sign on the door. I can't make out the name, but I think it starts with 'Ga'."

Joan went back to her book. "Yes. Galata."

"This could be a 'Cu' too," I said.

"Maybe Cutbank, then," Joan said. "Do you know anything else about the town you are looking for?"

"It was super small. Mostly an inn that doubled as a store. A few other buildings were there in the 50's when my Grandpa was there."

"I bet it's Galata. Not much there now, but Cutbank is much bigger. Both are on Highway 2."

I looked at Trey. "What do you think?"

Trey walked over to a giant wall map of Montana. "I think we can be there by tomorrow."

Eddie

His first day on the job at the hospital was unlike anything he had ever experienced. Dr. Ben told Eddie to go to the fifth floor and ask for Marylyn, the nurse who had been there when Stan died. Marylyn took Eddie to the personnel director for his picture I.D. and gave him the cafeteria pass. "This will give you any meal, as many times a day you like."

That little rectangle of laminated card stock with Eddie's name, picture, and the words "St. Mary's Cafeteria Pass" felt more precious than gold.

The picture on his I.D. card was not what he expected. He looked...good. When Eddie told the church ladies about Dr. Ben's job offer, they cheered with delight and then set to work on Eddie. Rosie's daughter was a hair stylist and she gave Eddie a fresh hair cut with scissors, not just clippers. Rosie then took Eddie to the store where Dorothy and Maggie met them in the men's section and insisted on choosing new shirts and pants for him.

Eddie felt ashamed, but Rosie recognized his reluctance and pulled him aside. "Don't you worry. This isn't charity."

"Sure feels that way," Eddie said.

"Nope. This is what a mother does for her son."

Eddie looked up from his worn shoes to Dorothy's green eyes.

"Edward, you fixed my car the other day. Your presence kept those ruffians away from Dorothy yesterday when you walked her to her car. Dr. Ben has recognized the Holy Spirit at work in you. Now, please, let us do something for you."

Wearing his new clothes and feeling as nervous as he did on the first day of school, Eddie looked in the mirror again. It was better, but not just right. The shirt was ironed with the landlady's borrowed iron and he had done a decent job of it, but he still looked…like Eddie.

In his journal, Jack had written that a new shirt always helped him to feel more confident. The mirror reflected a new shirt, but no confidence.

What do confident people look like? Eddie wondered. Thinking of clothing ads in the newspaper and on TV, Eddie pictured postures that enhanced the chiseled waistlines of men. Glancing at his belly, Eddie saw a stomach starved for food for decades, but not chiseled. The kind of posing in advertisements was not confidence, he decided. It was posing. Eddie was done posing.

Closing his eyes, he tried to think of Jack. Even though Jack had never written a description of himself in his journals, Eddie still had an image in his mind: tall and slender, brown hair and pale skin. Not one facial feature came to mind, but that didn't keep him from knowing Jack. It was his speech, his beliefs, his passions that Eddie knew and would recognize.

Keeping his eyes closed, Eddie straightened his back, pushed his shoulders down and away from his ears, lifted his chin. He sucked in his gut just a bit, but it was too difficult to breathe for long, so he decided that even confident people needed to lose a few pounds.

That is how Jack would stand. Tall and straight. Ready for the world. Face toward the horizon and walking with a genuine purpose.

Opening his eyes, Eddie saw a different man in the mirror. Even though the pressure of the world sat on his heart, Eddie saw a glimmer of determination in his reflection. The Eddie he saw had hope.

Now, dressed in the nicest clothes he had ever owned, he walked with pride to his new job. Marylyn showed Eddie around the fifth floor. "This wing is the Intensive Care Unit. Some of the patients are only allowed family visitors. I've gone to each room and asked the patients' families if they would like you to come and sit, pray or read with their loved ones. Here's a list of the rooms who said yes. As people come and go, Dr. Lawrence and I will update this list for you."

"That seems like a lot of work," Eddie said. "You have time to do that on top of everything else?"

"No," Marylyn laughed sweetly. "But it will be worth it. Prayer and company is sometimes better medicine than anything we can do."

Eddie's first visit was with a woman just out of heart surgery. She was eager to have a visitor and Eddie enjoyed talking to her. They had much in common, she had been a foster mother, but Eddie had never stayed with her. She drifted off to sleep while Eddie read to her, so he slipped out quietly, hoping to return again tomorrow and visit again.

The second person on the list was an old man who hadn't woken up in a week. "What can I do here?" Eddie asked Marylyn.

"Just read to him. We never know if in this state people can hear us or not, but I think we should assume that they can."

"Why?"

"If they can hear us and we don't speak to them, I imagine that would feel very lonely. If they can hear a voice, maybe it would be enough to pull them out of their sleep."

Eddie had never thought of it that way, but it was suddenly clear that of course that was true. If he thought about it more, it was what had happened to him. For years he had been asleep under the influence of bad choices and drugs. It was Jack Elliott's voice that had woken him, calling to him through the pages of the journals.

Eddie pulled a chair close to the old man's bed and started reading from First Samuel, one of Eddie's favorites with all the political plotting, the battles, the people doing very silly human things when God was right there. As he started the fourteenth chapter, a man walked into the room.

"Hello," he said. "You must be the man Marylyn told me would come and read."

"Eddie," he extended his hand.

"Henry." They shook hands. Eddie knew that he immediately liked Henry; he looked Eddie right in the eye, had a firm grip hand-shake, and didn't smile too widely. "The bible?" he pointed to Eddie's book.

"We were reading First Samuel."

"Ah," Henry nodded. "That is Jack's favorite."

The name tickled Eddie's spine. "His name is Jack?"

Henry nodded. "Greatest friend a man could ask for. Jack Elliott."

Eddie sat down. Hard. "Jack Elliott." This man, this wrinkled, still man lying in the bed had written the journals, the words, the stories that had reached out and pulled Eddie up by the hands. This sleeping man was the closest thing Eddie knew to a father, except for his new Father, and now he had the chance to meet him. If he would wake up, that is.

"Are you alright?" Henry asked.

No! Eddie thought. *I'm not alright. I've come face-to-face with the man who rescued me. He rescued me and doesn't even know it.* He didn't say any of that. "I'm fine. Just tired. I'll, um, I'll come back."

He ducked out of the room and went straight home, skipping dinner at the cafeteria.

Alison

After the museum and finding that picture, I felt the need for speed. The end of our journey seemed so close I could almost taste it. We were narrowing in on this woman, and despite the fear that she would pop my perfect image of Graypay, I also trusted Graypay enough to not have fallen in love with a complete monster. There had to be something about this woman that was special enough to send me after her. I just didn't know what that something special might be.

The roads in Montana were the picturesque road-trip roads I had always dreamed of: gentle hills, slowly winding roads and a view that truly didn't end until the horizon; it's all here in Montana, the greener side. The towns are little pockets of buildings clustered together every sixty miles or so. The space between is simply beautiful green space.

Our plan was to drive at least one more hour to the next town and find a hotel with two rooms. We called my parents and told them where we were. Mom told me Graypay was the same. Dad had gone back to Chicago for a few days to check on the deli, but was coming back soon. I told Henry about the museum. He knew the place and was glad we had found the photograph.

The next town had one small hotel, but only one room was available.

"Really?" Trey asked the clerk at the little store that sold groceries and clothing and also manned the hotel with three rooms.

"It's a regular rush on us tonight," the man said. "My wife's family is over from Idaho and takin' two rooms. You want the other?"

Trey and I exchanged a very uncomfortable look. "No," I said. "We'll head to the next town."

"You're choice," the man shrugged.

"What do you think we'll find in Galata?" I asked as we drove toward the next town.

"Hopefully a really hot older woman who will readily agree to drive a few hundred miles away with two perfect strangers to see a man she used to be in love with."

I made a face, "A hot older woman? Really?"

Trey laughed. "Why not?"

"She's probably married and perfectly happy. What if we bring up a really painful past and ruin her life?"

"You think too much," Trey teased.

"Seriously. It could stir up some really bad memories for her."

"Yeah, it could. Should we turn around or risk it?"

If we turned around, this woman's past would remain her past and nothing bad or unexpected would happen. No, I realized, the unexpected always happens. Losing the journals and the car accident were complete surprises. If we kept going and did find this woman, then what? That would be a complete surprise.

Choosing to continue offered the promise of solving this mystery, no matter what the consequences. Turning back would offer us the safety of not taking the risk. It also assured that I would forever regret not seeing this to the end. "We

236

should keep going. If we stir up bad memories for her, then Graypay isn't the man I thought he was."

"I don't think Graypay would send you to find a woman from his past if their relationship was terrible."

"Then why did they break up at all?" I wondered. "If he's been pining for her all these years, why didn't they get married?"

Trey glanced at me quickly. "That would be the 'mystery' part."

"Argh!" I shook off the emotion of doubt as best I could. "This is so frustrating! I'm not normally this…stupid. I keep second guessing this whole trip and worrying about what we'll find."

"That's just human."

"I don't like it."

Trey smiled, "I can't believe I'm about to say this, but I think that's why Graypay planned this trip: to shake up your understanding of what life is all about. You put yourself out there to do something great. Sometimes it works and sometimes it doesn't. Either way, you have to keep trying until you find what's right." He laughed. "Like the Hokey Pokey. That's what it's all about."

I shook my head in disbelief. "You are equating the great mystery of life to the Hokey Pokey?"

"You put your neck in, you put your neck out, you put your neck in and shake it all about…" He looked at me, "You're putting your neck out to find this woman for your grandfather. You're doing it out of love." He looked back to the road. "*That's* what it all about."

Red Letter Day

June 1957
Jack Elliott

"Oh, Jack," Mrs. Miller started to cry as she finished reading the letter. "I'm so sorry."

I didn't want her to be sorry. I wanted her to tell me that I didn't need to bring Minnie back. After all, I had taken good care of her all this time.

"Jack," she reached for my hand.

I pulled away. "No. There must be a way for me to keep her. She's mine."

"No, darlin'. She's not." Mrs. Miller spoke kindly, but the words sliced my soul to shreds.

"I love her!"

"We all do. But her family is there now. They want her back."

The letter in my hand ruined my future with Minnie. Mrs. Miller pulled me to a chair and told me to sit down before I fell over. She called for Mr. Miller and he ran over, thinking I had taken ill.

I had.

I did not have a stone heart, but one made of thorns and sour berries. Minnie's laughter drifted through the window and I watched her swing with her head tipped back and her mouth wide with a delighted scream.

"How can I do this now?" I asked. "She's my life." How could I take her back? My mind clouded over as I imagined leaving Montana without her. How would I fill my days? It was for her that I woke up in the morning and it was her rolling giggle that filled me with complete joy. At night we shared star stories. Recently, Minnie started to make up her own and while they wandered with no clear beginning or end, they all had the same idea: two stars that traveled through the night sky looking for a place to stay. The night before Minnie started school, we snuck out after midnight for star stories.

"My turn," she announced and without waiting for me to respond, she started her short story. "The two stars were very tired one day after shining brightly all night for the earth people. So they decided to take a nap in a field of star-daisies. The little star slept a little while, but was bored of it. She wanted to surprise her big star with some star daisies, so she got up and collected them. But the daisies didn't stay happy. Their heads fell over and the little star knew they were thirsty. There is always water in a town, so the little star walked to the town to give her thirsty star-daisies a drink. She wanted them to be happy when she gave them to the big star "

She stopped talking and I thought for a moment she had talked herself to sleep. In all honesty, I desperately wanted her to finish the story; this was the first time she had talked about that day on the way here when she wandered off. "What did the little star find in town?" I prompted her.

"Other little stars with a tea set. A real pretty one."

I smiled. "And the little star forgot about the big star?"

"Maybe. She didn't mean to."

"I know. Did the big star get angry with the little star?"

"Yes. And he punished her by not giving her any pudding."

In reality, I hadn't punished Minnie at all for wandering away, but because I bought sleeper car tickets for the rest of the trip, I didn't have enough money to buy her pudding the next day in the dining car. Apparently that had been a severe enough punishment to make it all the way into a star story.

The thought of never having star stories with her again weakened my knees.

CHAPTER 19

Small World

June 25th
Trey

Alison pounded on my hotel room door.

"I just got off the phone with my mom. When Dad got home yesterday there was a letter from a church here in Montana. The priest was responding to a letter that Graypay sent a few months ago. About someone named Minnie."

"Who's Minnie?"

She thumped me on the forehead with her finger. "HER!"

"Minnie? How could a priest, or anyone, know it's the right person?" I asked. "I don't want to be a doubting Thomas, but Graypay's letters could not have described her. He hadn't seen her in decades."

"The priest said that he couldn't reveal how he knew because it was something shared during a bible study and he didn't want to breach any confidences. Mom said he sounded quite certain that he knew where she was. It's possible this is her!"

"So we drive farther on a possibility?" I asked, thinking of how tired I was.

"We've gone farther on less than this," Alison shrugged. "Why not?"

"Sure," I moaned. "Why not?" I unfolded the map. "Where in Montana?"

"Chinook."

I looked up and smiled. "We are in Chinook."

"I already called the church. They are closed of course," Alison threw her cell phone on the bed and sat down looking completely dejected.

"Al, it's after six. We'll go in the morning."

"I know. It's just that we are so close. Tomorrow morning seems too long to wait."

"Let's start filling the time we have between now and when they open the church by getting some dinner."

Alison looked at me with a strained expression. "How can you possibly be thinking of food right now?"

"It's easy with my stomach rumbling. Come on. My treat."

She rolled her eyes. "It's always your treat. You have the credit card."

The diner had a few tables and an atmosphere of coming home for dinner. The tables were covered with different types of table clothes; checkered, flowered or striped, creating a picnic feel. None of the silverware matched and the glasses were the red Coca-Cola glasses that I remembered from when I was a kid. Each table had four chairs, but a stack of another dozen chairs stood in the corner in case customers were plentiful. Scents of French fries and grilled meat greeted my nose and reinvigorated my empty stomach. From behind the counter, a young woman waved and called out, "Just take a seat anywhere. You both want Cokes?"

We nodded and took a table in the corner.

"What do you think of this place?" I asked Alison, wondering what her opinion of such a haphazardly decorated restaurant would be after growing up with parents who took great time and effort in the physical atmosphere of their deli and restaurant.

"Homey. I like it."

"Really?"

"I'm not as fussy as my parents. I don't mind this," she pointed to the mismatched silverware.

The woman came over with two icy Cokes and took our order. The server was not what Alison's parents would deem an appropriately dressed. Her black hair was streaked with purple highlights, several earrings studded her ears and her eye make-up was on the heavy side. All in all, she was cute. A little older than me, maybe, but cute. Too colorful for my tastes, though. While we waited for our food, Alison took out the cigar box and spread everything out again, like she did every night.

"Again?" I asked. "We're going to the church tomorrow."

"I just want to make sure we have our information right."

"Alison, any information we think we know is mostly based on guessing." She gave me the 'look'. "Ok, *educated* guessing. Let's just wait and enjoy a dinner that doesn't involve a mystery."

"Hmmm."

"Hmmm…what?"

"You're probably right," she said. I couldn't believe my ears! "But I just get the strangest feeling that we are still missing something."

I caved and reviewed what we thought we knew. "So, Graypay comes to Montana right after leaving home. We know that because…"

"He told me those stories," Alison finished.

"Right. And we came here looking for a woman because…"

"He told me," She paused and sighed. "He told me to in a dream."

"Right. We think she will have black hair because of that lock," I pointed to it laying on the table.

"And we know her name," Alison smiled. "Minnie."

The waitress came over and interrupted, "Did you need something?"

We both shook our heads. She looked confused, but smiled again, "Your food should be up soon." Noticing the clutter on the table, she inquired about it. "A project?"

"A mystery," Alison said. "I'm looking for someone who used to know my grandfather."

"Sounds intriguing," the waitress said. "And what is all this?" she motioned to the pictures, the newspaper clippings.

"These are the clues we have to find her," I said. "It's a really a long story, but the short version is this: we started with the hope of solving a mystery, but most of our clues were stolen. We've come from Chicago here looking for someone named Minnie whom we hope is still in Montana and still in contact with her church otherwise our trip tomorrow will be pointless."

"This church?" the waitress pointed to the picture of the white-steeple church.

"No. The church here in town." Alison answered.

"And what do you want with her?"

Alison sighed. "Just to let her know that Graypay has been looking for her for a long time. I don't know why or how they separated, but I do know that she was important enough to him to send us in search of her. Maybe she would come with us to the hospital where Graypay is. Maybe that would settle his mind."

"Graypay?" the waitress asked. "Nickname?"

Alison smiled. "From me, actually. It's how I used to say 'grandpa'. It stuck. His name is Jack. Jack Elliott."

The cook called, "Order up!" and our server gasped. "And tomorrow you are going to the church to meet with a priest who might know this Minnie?"

Alison nodded. "I just hope he does. I don't know where to go after this."

"I see." It surprised me that even our waitress was a little teary-eyed at our story. "I'll go bring your meals."

Eddie

Stan died owning nothing. Eddie didn't have enough for a funeral. Stan never talked about family. It wasn't until the nurse asked Eddie about contacting Stan's family that Eddie realized he didn't really know Stan at all. They were both foster kids. That's why they had remained friends all these years, but it was an unspoken rule that they didn't discuss where they had come from.

Where had he grown up? Did he have brothers or sisters?

Lou didn't know either.

Eddie said his good-bye at the hospital. There was no need for a funeral, which was fine with Eddie. Stan knew a handful of people and owed them all money. It was better that he just slip away to the next life, whatever that might be, and that Eddie just move on with his.

Easier said than done.

For a moment after he heard knocking at the door, Eddie had forgotten what happened two days ago and expected Stan to be standing at the door with a six-pack. Of course, it wasn't Stan. It was Lou.

"You busy, man?" Lou said, looking nervously up and down the hall.

"Naw," Eddie left the door open and walked back to his chair.

"You didn't show up for cards last night." Lou sat down at the tippy dining room table.

Eddie closed one of Jack's journals and shook his head. "Wasn't feelin' up to it."

"Yeah. Me neither."

Eddie scoffed. "Then how'd you know I wasn't there?"

"Oh, I was there but left early."

Eddie nodded and shifted in his chair. "They all know about Stan?"

Lou wiped his nose on the back of his hand. "Yeah. But," he paused for a long moment, "they wasn't there, ya' know? They didn't see it all."

Eddie understood. Stan had been really broken. More broken than Eddie had ever seen, and he'd seen a lot of broken things: bodies, fingers, families.

"They talked about him, the guys," Lou continued. "They said some nice things about Stan for a while."

"For a while?" Eddie wondered what they talked about.

"Well, you know Stan. He wasn't one to keep many friends."

Eddie chuckled. "We're all out a few bucks, huh?"

Lou laughed with him, but it was short. "They talked about why you don't come 'round."

"What'd you tell 'em?"

"Nothin."

Eddie waited for Lou to continue.

"You did somethin' with that water."

"I baptized him."

"But he still died. It didn't help him at all."

"I think it did."

247

"But God? You really believe that God would have healed Stan? Stan, the man who stole and borrowed money and never paid it back?"

"I don't understand it all," Eddie said as he picked up one of Jack's notebooks, "but I've read that sometimes things happen and God is there and the good of the moment isn't seen until later."

"The guys were right," Lou frowned at Eddie. "You changed."

"I know."

"You comin' to be one o' them believers?"

Eddie smiled. "Seems like it."

"How come? I mean, Stan died. God didn't save him."

Eddie stared at the kitchen sink, not seeing it but remembering the flames from that first page of burning notebook that seared his mind. "I think God did."

"But he died!" Lou repeated.

"Yeah. Ya' know, though, his last thought was about God. Maybe he was saved." Eddie leaned forward. "You want to risk a new life?"

Lou scoffed. "You mean change my ways? Become an honest man?"

Eddied nodded.

Lou shook his head. "Naw, man. Too late for me. Old dog, new tricks. You know how it is."

Eddie handed Lou the first of Jack's journals. "I'm not sayin' that the answer to all of your problems will be right there for the takin' if you read these notebooks. My problems are still kickin'. But there is something about this man who wrote in these notebooks that has helped me see my life in a way that doesn't seem so...lost."

Lou eyed the notebook as if the pages had fangs and thirsted for his beer-steeped blood. "This notebook can change my life?"

"No. But you can take the first step."

The Last Star Story

June 1957
Jack Elliott

Our last star story was bitter. The blanket felt prickly and Minnie was extra sleepy from all the energy she spent at school. "Come on, Minnie," I hoisted her out of bed. "The stars are ready."

"Not tonight." She rolled over.

"We have to, tonight," I said, glancing over at our packed bags.

"Why?"

"They are telling the last story."

She sat up at this announcement. "Why?"

"Because tomorrow you and I have to leave."

She pulled the blankets up around her. "I don't want to leave."

"The stars will explain it all. Come on."

The October air was extra cold, so instead of lying down on the blanket, I wrapped it around me and kept Minnie on my lap where I knew she would be warmer.

I began.

"Just a few years ago, a little girl was born and her parents were very happy. She was just a speck of a child, but her eyes were bright, her hair shiny black, and she found happiness in everything. Then something bad happened. A fire crept into that family's home, destroying everything except the little girl."

"Even her parents?" Minnie asked.

"Yes. Even her parents. You see fire is a creature that doesn't know good or bad, right or wrong. It just knows its own hunger. Fire will eat anything it can. Sometimes, when people are careful, the fire helps them with warmth and cooking. Sometimes the fire jumps out of its place and starts a big mess that can hurt people. That's what happened."

"What happened to the little girl?"

"A kind man and wife took her in. Their son returned home to help." My voice stuck as I remembered the letter from Ruthie and the last words Jacob spoke to me: *Live well. I love you.*

Minnie wiggled and turned to face me. "This is my story."

I could only nod.

"Does it have a happy ending?"

"It's not over yet." I steadied my nerves. "Before they left Montana, the son sent letters to all kinds of churches, lawyers, and police officers to look for the girl's family. This week the son got a letter saying that her family is there. Back in Montana where they used to live."

"Do I have to go back?" she asked, her voice as small as she.

The dreams of running away with her, keeping her all to myself vanished. Until this moment, I was going to tell her that we could leave here and hide so she could be my little girl and I could be her daddy instead of her Jack-Jack. But that would be wrong and I knew it. "We do have to go back."

"They will be strangers."

"Only for a while. You and I were strangers once too. Now we love each other. It will be the same way." I hoped that was true.

"I don't want to go."

"I don't either," I admitted.

"Can we run away?"

"If we did that, I would be a kidnapper."

She rested her head on my shoulder. "And that would be bad."

So true. I would readily commit that crime if I truly thought it was the right thing for Minnie. Until I saw her family, I was going on the assumption that they really wanted her. The letter didn't say if they were an aunt or uncle or cousin, just that they did want her back.

We left the next morning. I had enough money to buy plane tickets, but I wanted the slower pace of the train. Every minute that ticked by was another minute closer to giving Minnie up.

I splurged on everything: the sleeper car, extra pudding in the dining car, even a new dress for Minnie for the last day on the train. If I was going to give her away to family, they would at least see that she was well cared for.

All too soon, we arrived back home in Montana. Just as I had hoped, nothing in town had changed. Mr. and Mrs. Thompson were there to meet us. Minnie was shy with them at first, not remembering them well, but she quickly warmed up to them and was soon clinging to Mrs. Thompson's hand.

"Are they here?" I asked.

Mr. Thompson nodded. "At the bed and breakfast."

"How are they related? Do you know?"

"From what I could gather," Mr. Thompson kept his voice low, "the wife is the little one's aunt."

I could feel my face growing hot as tears seemed to form just under every inch of skin in the form of sweat. "Alright," I said, putting on a strong face and turning to Minnie. "Your family is here. Let's go meet them."

She let go of Mrs.Thompson's hand and ran into my arms. "I don't want to."

"I know. They are your mother's family."

"I don't know her," Minnie said and buried her face on my shoulder.

"You will," I tried to sound convincing. "Just like we talked about. They will be strangers at first, but they are your family. They will love you and you will grow up beautifully."

Minnie said nothing, so I carried her to the bed and breakfast. The couple was sitting uncomfortably in the parlor, looking at the coffee as if it were poisoned. Mrs. Baker, the proprietor of the little Inn was doing her best to entertain them, but there was obviously a language barrier. As we walked in, the husband stood up stiffly and barked a few choppy words at his wife. She stood and bowed to me. "I am Sing-Lou."

"I'm Jack," I said. "I'm glad to meet you." That wasn't true at all, but manners show up at the least likely times. "This is Minnie." I turned Minnie around so she could see her aunt and uncle. She gripped me tighter.

The husband spoke again, his temper not impressed by my manners at all. Then Sing-Lou blushed and nodded

"Is there something wrong?" I asked.

"My husband never like her father," she pointed to Minnie.

"He doesn't want her?" I asked, feeling suddenly hopeful.

"Family honor. We must take."

"I do want to keep her," I said. "I've been taking care of her and, well," I looked at Minnie and smiled, "she really is something special."

Sing-Lou looked abashed. She spoke to her husband and he glared at me. Stomping his way across the room, he plucked Minnie right out of my arms, shouted and pushed Minnie into Sing-Lou's arms.

I was so stunned, I just stood there like a dope and let it all happen.

Sing-Lou, over the sound of Minnie's screaming, said, "He say, no thank you."

And she left.

I followed them outside yelling, "Wait! At least let me say good-bye."

The husband was irritated with me and he waved his hands, directing me to go away. He shouted and carried on as much as I did.

"I just want to say good-bye," I yelled again and again, hoping that by repetition alone he would begin to understand.

Sing-Lou had put Minnie in a car with two people in the front seat. The person in the passenger seat reached back and kept Minnie from running back to me. Mr. Sing-Lou was now just inches away and his spittle coated my face. He didn't back off until Sing-Lou put her arm on his and spoke to him. He had one more thing to say, which despite his repetition, didn't mean a thing.

"We go," Sing-Lou said. "You stay."

Mr. Miller held me back while Mrs. Miller pushed Minnie's suitcase into Sing-Lou's arms. "That young man took good care of her. A proper good-bye isn't too much to ask."

Sing-Lou looked tormented. Her husband yelled again and Sing-Lou jumped and hustled to the car.

And then she was gone.

CHAPTER 20

A Mini Surprise

June 26th
Alison

Our drive to the church was short. We could have walked the eight blocks, but my knees were knocking together so badly, Trey insisted we drive. Before meeting the priest, I went in the church and lit a candle for Graypay, praying to the Virgin Mother that she also pray for Graypay. I lit another candle for Trey, who had followed me with little more than sketchy clues and was becoming a fierce friend not just a troublesome boy. I lit another candle for the woman for whom we searched. I didn't know what to pray for her, but I knew that God would know best what she needed and that would be my prayer also.

"Ready?" Trey asked.

"No. Let's go."

The priest had listened to the message I left the night before and was expecting us.

"Father Jim," he introduced himself. "I understand you've been on quite a journey." He was wearing his collar and black suit, with his hair neatly combed and face freshly shaven. The rectory office smelled of fresh coffee, which I eagerly accepted. He seemed as nervous as I felt.

"That's putting it lightly," Trey chuckled. "This is Alison Elliott. It was her grandfather who sent you the letter."

I was stupidly silent during these introductions. We were finally here, in contact with someone who might actually know who we were looking for. Perhaps this was Minnie's parish, her home church where she came every Sunday to worship.

Father Jim shifted his weight. "There is someone I would like to introduce you to. Minnie?" A young woman stepped out of Father Jim's office and joined us. Her familiar face knocked the wind out of me as though Father Jim had swung a chair into my gut.

"You…" I stammered. "You were our waitress last night."

She nodded. "I saw the cigar box, the hair. So many memories came flooding back, I couldn't say anything."

"That's why you left?" Trey asked, remembering that a different waitress had cleared our plates and brought the bill.

"I had to get home and check."

"No," I said, sounding more angry than in shock. "You can't be Minnie. Graypay is old. You are just a little older than me. This isn't right."

"This will take some explaining," the fake Minnie said. Reaching into her purse, she took out a few yellowing photographs. "These should help."

Graypay's youthful face looked at me from the photographs. He was holding a tiny little girl with black hair on his lap. Both were dressed in their Sunday best and sitting quite formally; not smiling. A true old-fashioned picture. The next photo was less formal. The little black-haired girl had her arms around Graypay's neck, their cheeks squished together as they both smiled widely for the photographer.

"I don't understand. This can't be you."

"That's my mother."

"She's just a little girl," I laughed. Father Jim and Minnie both looked at me oddly. "Sorry. This is just, well, this is another mystery."

"And a good story,

by the sounds of it," Father Jim said, indicating chairs. "Let's be comfortable while all this comes together."

Minnie started. "My mother's name is Meifeng, but for a time when she was a little girl, the man who cared for her called her Minnie. Her parents had died in a fire and an elderly couple took her in. Mother could never remember their names, but said they were kind and loving. Living with them was a man, their son, named Jack. It was Jack that cared for her the most. But a few years after Jack took her in, my mother's family from China found her and took her as their own daughter. It was then that she returned to her given name of Meifeng, but she always preferred Minnie. When I was born, that is what she named me. Minnie." Her face turned dark. "When I heard you speaking last night, I panicked. Why are you looking for my mother?"

My turn. I told her about my life list and the purpose of the cross-country trip, how it was complicated by Graypay's Alzheimer's and interrupted by the car accident. I showed her the cigar box and the contents and told her about the picture Trey and I found at the museum. "My grandfather just wanted to see Minnie, or Meifeng, one last time. I'm not sure why, but I would guess he wants to make sure she's... that she's okay. I think he would like her to come with us to the hospital to see him."

"The hospital in North Dakota?" Minnie asked.

"Do you think your mother would? Can you bring her?" I asked.

Minnie glanced at Father Jim. "No."

"You haven't even asked her. Does she know that we are looking for her? Did you call her?"

Minnie shook her head. "No. My mother spoke often of Jack and often wished she could see him again. Cancer took her two years ago."

I had no words for this. Was she really saying what I thought she was saying?

Trey eventually found his voice. "You mean…the woman we've been looking for is dead?"

Father Jim put his hand on Minnie's shoulder. "Meifeng's death has been very difficult for Minnie. Her father died years ago."

"I'm sorry," I said. "I… I hope we haven't… we don't mean to make you upset."

"I'm happy you are here and that you've spent so much time looking for her. That means that Jack really did love her."

"Did she ever doubt that?" Trey asked.

"When her aunt and uncle took her back, my mother was only five or six years old. My aunt never liked to talk of those years, her niece being raised by a single white man and all. My mother never forgot Jack, but there were many times when she wondered if he gave her up easily or if it was difficult for him. She told me that for several years, she had convinced herself that he was nothing but a ghost memory, you know, a result of the trauma of losing her parents, that maybe she had made him

258

up completely. But then, when her aunt died, she found those pictures. Then she knew.

"When I saw that lock of hair last night, it all fell into place. He had loved her so much, that he kept that all these years. I wish my mother could have known that."

I didn't know what to do or say.

"I brought you this," she handed me a large envelope. "I made copies of the pictures my mother found after her aunt died. I included some of the pictures of her childhood and wedding pictures and some from my childhood. Maybe that will help your grandfather."

My voice wouldn't work, so Trey thanked her for me and made an excuse to leave.

So What Was the Point?

Trey

There wasn't much to say after that. Conversation dwindled quickly and, noticing Alison's silence, I said that we had taken up enough of their time and should leave. Minnie looked a little sad that we would be leaving so soon. A connection with her mother's past was probably thrilling for her; almost like having her mother back for a while. I admit that the disappointment of learning that the woman we had been seeking had been dead for two years was heavy. We needed to absorb everything, process our loss...whatever people say when they feel completely overwhelmed...and decide how to tell Graypay. That is, if Graypay was awake and if he would even remember that he had sent us on a mission to find Minnie.

Now that we had proof that there was a woman in Graypay's past, although she wasn't a woman at the time, I knew that Alison's dream had been real. Of course, dreams are real when they happen inside your mind, but to think that Graypay had really spoken to Alison in a dream gave me goose bumps.

Neither of us spoke all the way back to the highway. We didn't talk about where to go next, but I naturally headed east. If we drove and didn't stop to tour any museums or search for churches, we could be back at the hospital by sometime tomorrow.

While Alison remained quiet in her thoughts, I wondered if our trip had been a success or a complete failure. We had found Minnie, but two years too late. We had followed every clue we had, solved the mystery of who she was, and had pictures from her daughter to show him. Would it be enough?

We drove for almost three hours before I finally broke the silence. "Are you okay?"

Alison shrugged. "I feel like I've lost everything. My cross-country trip was upset when the journals were stolen and then destroyed when we crashed. Graypay is still unconscious. Minnie is dead. I don't know what to think."

I knew that this was delicate waters for me to tread: a girl who thinks she's lost everything plus a boy who habitually, yet unintentionally, says the wrong thing, equals the most uncomfortable ride back to the hospital where potentially more bad news awaits. Play it safe. "What would Graypay say?" *There*, I thought, *take a dose of your own medicine*. Besides, if I couldn't think of the right thing to say, maybe Alison would say if for me.

"Find the good in the situation," Alison sighed a let her head fall back into the headrest. "I always thought that was stupid, especially when all I want to do is stew in my disappointment."

"It's good that you still had your cross-country trip."

"It was supposed to be all the way to the Pacific Ocean."

"Is this your last cross-country trip?" I asked.

"I hope not."

"Well, next time then." I tried to think of another positive. "We solved the mystery."

"Yeah." Alison obviously was not going to bite down hard on the glass-is-half-full concept.

"And Minnie seemed to appreciate knowing that her mother was loved by Jack."

She sighed slowly. "Trey, it's just not the happy ending I thought we would have." I could feel her looking at me as I drove. It was nice. "I had this idea that we would find this woman and she would be thrilled to hear that Graypay was looking for her. She would come with us to the hospital and he would wake up and remember."

Similar dreams had sifted through my mind too. "I thought she would be an old, gray-hair bachelorette who had never married for her love for Graypay."

Alison giggled. "How very romantic of you."

"It's actually a movie plot that my mom watches constantly." I glanced at Alison. "Look," I pointed to a billboard, "There's a restaurant in a few miles. Let's stop for dinner and take a look at the pictures she gave us."

Eddie

Eddie stood at the door, the box in his hands. He couldn't tell if Jack Elliott was awake, so he walked in quietly.

Jack stirred and startled when he saw he wasn't alone. "You aren't a nurse," Jack said.

Those were not the first words Eddie wanted Jack Elliott to say to him, but he supposed you don't always get what you want when loitering in doorways. He cleared his throat, "Um, no sir."

Jack eyed Eddie critically. "Are you lost? You look too well to be a patient."

Eddie smiled. "No, sir. My name is Eddie Barkley. I have your box." He held it up a little.

"My journals," Jack smiled and sat up a little straighter. "You found them. The police didn't tell me they had been found."

Eddie's face prickled hot. Police.

They aren't here, are they? No, he told himself, *that is the old way of thinking. Forgiveness. Seek forgiveness from this man. If I'm arrested, I deserve it.* "I found them," Eddie said, pleased that what he said was true. He had found them in the truck of Jack Elliott's car when he robbed it. *No,* he scolded himself, *That's still the old way.* In his mind he recited *Psalm 15:2 "He whose walk is blameless and who does what is righteous, who speaks the truth from his heart."*

"Mr. Elliott," Eddie started his rehearsed speech. "I've read your journals. I'm sorry if I've crossed a line," he added quickly when Jack's mouth dropped open, "but until I read them, I was a bad man. I never hurt nobody, but there's been other stuff I've done. Stuff I'm not proud of. Your journals," Eddie felt his throat tighten, "they showed me a new way of thinking and living. I've read about your life and I want to be like you. A good man."

There. He had said it. Now it had to be true. Jack stared at Eddie. As the silence lingered, Eddie shifted his weight and realized he was still holding the box. He walked to a table under the window and set it down.

Eddie knew what he needed to say, but it was harder than he thought. His palms were sweatier now than when he had pried the trunk open. He felt more exposed standing here under Jack's stare than when he walked passed a surveillance camera.

"So, Mr. Elliott, I want to say I'm sorry and all."

"Sorry for what?" Jack asked. "Returning my journals?"

Eddie forced himself to look Jack in the eyes. "I was the one what took 'em, see? I saw that beautiful box in your trunk an' figured there'd be some pawning goods."

Jack sighed and nodded. "I see." Then smiling the way Eddie imagined he smiled when Minnie told her star stories. "Quite a disappointment, I'm sure, to see nothing but notebooks."

Eddie laughed, "It sure was."

Jack's face darkened and Eddie was certain he would call a nurse to call the police. Eddie spoke, "Mr. Elliott, I know I've done wrong. If you see fit to call the cops, I won't run."

"I wrote those journals so my memories would not disappear, as if I could trap my life between pen and paper. You've read them, you know what's happening to my mind."

Eddied nodded and Jack continued, "When they were stolen, I

realized that nothing I do can save my past. Nothing will keep my mind from slipping into this void. Now, you're telling me that through my journals you found salvation?"

"Yes, sir," Eddie nodded. He wanted to stand and shout to Jack Elliott all the wonderful things he had seen since Christ opened his eyes, all the trouble he's had from friends who didn't understand. Not yet, anyway. He wanted to tell Jack he had no idea where his life would go from here, but he knew that Jesus would care for his soul. He didn't say any of those things. Something kept him silent.

"Do you have a Bible?" Jack asked Eddie.

"Yes, sir." He held up the Bible from Ben.

"Good. Good," Jack said. "I will not call the police, Mr. Barkley. Thank you for returning my journals."

Eddie smiled and turned for the door. "I hope you feel better real soon, Mr. Elliott."

"Eddie," Jack called. "Before you go, will you read to me?"

A nurse walked in as Eddie was reading from the Gospel of Mark.

"Oh," the nurse smiled at Eddie, "Have you been here long?"

Eddie didn't have a watch, but he guessed it had been at least an hour. Maybe longer. "I'm not sure. I've just been reading to him."

"Are you a volunteer?" the nurse asked.

"No, ma'am. Just a friend."

"You knew Mr. Elliott?"

Eddie shrugged, suddenly feeling shy. "Yes, but this is the first time I'd met him."

The nurse obviously didn't understand, but let it go. "Well, thank you for reading to him. It's wonderful to have someone

265

with him. His family went to rest this afternoon, but they'll be back soon I believe."

Eddie wanted to run out of that hospital room before someone who really knew Jack walked in and saw the journals returned. "That's good. Family is best."

"Even now, it's good for him to have company. I'm sure he knows he's not alone."

Now Eddie frowned.

The nurse saw his confusion and explained, "A man in this state may still be able to hear people talking. He might be able to feel someone holding his hand. It's important for loved ones to do what they can."

"I've heard that." Eddie said. "He's just asleep now, isn't he?"

"He's in a coma," the nurse said. "Has been for over a week."

Eddie was glad he was still sitting down, for his face felt red hot and his hands trembled. The nurse walked around Jack's bed and put her hand on Eddie's shoulder. "Are you alright? You look like you might fall right out of your chair."

It was then when Eddie noticed that Jack was lying down and sound asleep. More than that, there was a breathing tube and a beeping heart monitor. He hadn't noticed those before; perhaps he was so nervous about returning the journals that he didn't really see what was right in front of him.

Trey

After ordering burgers, fries and Cokes, the meal of champions who have both won the battle and lost the war, we sat staring out at a tiny parking lot.

"Thank you," Alison said.

"For what?"

"Everything. Agreeing to drive us across the country, helping Graypay when he was lost, driving me to Montana and back." She paused and looked down at her hands. "When Graypay first told me you would be joining us, I was really mad. He was right though," she looked at me, "you were the right person."

"I need to say thank you, too. This trip has really opened my eyes."

She nodded, her eyes moist. "I'm glad."

The 'moment' was interrupted by our server. "Here's a few nickels," she set a stack of four coins on the table. "Why don't you two pop these babies into the box and fill this place with some tunes?"

Alison smiled. "Go ahead."

Following orders, I grabbed the nickels and walked to the juke box. I expected it to be filled with CDs, but this was an original, with vinyl records: the greatest hits from the 1950's all the way through the mid-1980's. The music began after a series of mechanical arms clicked the record into place, sending Nat King Cole's 'Unforgettable' into the atmosphere.

"I like this song," Alison said. "Graypay and I used to dance to this one at night."

"I know," I held out my hand. "Come on."

She blushed and looked around. "Here? We're in a diner."

"I know," I smiled, enjoying Alison's nervousness. She hesitated only a moment and then took my hand. I had watched Alison and Graypay dance, but I had always refused to join them mostly because I didn't want to dance with a man and I was too shy to dance with Alison. My excuse was always that they would dance and I would be the audience. It was awkward as I took her hand and put my other hand on her back, but that feeling didn't last long.

When we left the diner, it was dark. I bought a tall coffee to go and told Alison I would drive all night. Even though we were empty handed, we wanted to get back to Graypay. At two o'clock in the morning, I pulled over to stretch my legs. "Alison," I woke her. "Look."

We both climbed out of the car and looked up. "The Milky Way," she sighed. "Finally."

CHAPTER 21

Follow the Fly-Bees

June 28
Trey

Mrs. Elliott called my parents to let them know Alison and I had returned safely. My mother thought I had been at the hospital all that time. Mrs. Elliott was furious with me for not telling my parents.

"I'm sorry," I felt the shame behind my eyes. I didn't know what to say. I didn't tell my parents because of the way the conversation had gone between my mother and I when she told me they wouldn't be coming. Alison had I had been gone for six days and they never once called me or Mrs. Elliott. "I was wrong to not tell them."

Mrs. Elliott studied my face. Her lips were pressed together and her eyes narrowed. "It's okay." She said. "We knew you were safe. You took good care of Alison. Thank you."

Mr. Elliott had been behind me, listening. He came up and put an arm around my shoulder. "Come on, son. Let's go sit with Graypay and hear about your trip."

We turned to go into Graypay's room, but stopped dead in our tracks when Alison, Henry, Father Jim, and a very nervous Minnie walked around the corner.

"Mom, Dad," Alison was holding Minnie's hand. "This is Father Jim, the one who contacted you about Graypay's letter." Mr. and Mrs. Elliott shook his hand. "This is Minnie. She is the one we found. Her mother, well," Alison looked at Minnie, "Graypay took care of Minnie's mother when she was little. That's who he sent us to find."

Mr. Elliott stood staring at this young woman with jet black and purple hair. "It was your mother's hair in the box?"

"How did you know about that?" Alison asked.

"I peeked in that box once when I was a kid," Mr. Elliott confessed. "That lock of hair has haunted my imagination for decades. Your mother?"

Minnie nodded. "My mother's parents were killed in a fire and Jack took her in. He cared for her until my aunt and her family came to find them. Then Jack had to give her up."

"Sounds like quite a story," Mrs. Elliott said.

"Yeah," Alison sighed. "A story that was almost completely lost. His journals would have been a huge help."

"Oh! They're back!" Mrs. Elliott exclaimed. "Two days ago, when your dad and I went down to the cafeteria for lunch, someone brought the chest back. All the journals are inside."

"Really?" Alison and I said at the same time.

Before we could get any more information from Mrs. Elliott, a nurse ran up to us, crying. "He's awake!"

We froze.

"Can we see him?" I asked.

270

"Soon. The doctor is removing the ventilator and will spend a few minutes with him." She hugged Mrs. Elliott and quickly returned to Graypay's room to help.

We all waited, pacing the halls, crying for joy. The strange mix of emotion was enchanting. Minnie was here, Graypay was awake, and the mystery was solved.

The nurse motioned from Graypay's door that we could come in. Like a parade of ballerina's, we tip-toed into his room, totally disregarding the two visitors at a time rule, and stared at Graypay. He was indeed awake, though obviously not understanding what was going on.

Minnie looked uncomfortable. "This should just be family. I'll wait outside."

"Nonsense," Mr. Elliott said. "Come on." He took Minnie's hand and walked up to the bed. "Dad?"

Graypay's eyes focused slowly on his son. "You're here," his voice was very weak.

Mr. Elliott smiled. "Of course. How are you feeling?"

"Drugged. Where's Alison?"

"I'm here," she walked up to the bed.

Graypay studied her face and watched as her tears streamed down her cheeks and dripped onto his blanket. "I'm sorry I ruined your trip."

"You didn't, Graypay. Trey and I just got back from Galata."

His eyes widened. "Gala—Galata. How did you --?"

"Your cigar box. I found it and we followed the clues."

Graypay's heart rate monitor started beeping faster and the nurse nervously whispered to Alison that he needed to calm down.

"Graypay, it's okay. We found her. But —" she hesitated and I understood why. Telling him now that Minnie was dead, now when he was so frail, would possibly cause more problems.

"And she brought me with her," Minnie spoke up.

Graypay looked toward Minnie. Seconds ticked by as he studied her face. Then recognition lit his eyes and he smiled. "My Minnie," he breathed.

"I'm here." Minnie took his hand.

I couldn't believe my ears. She was playing the role of her mother, giving Graypay his greatest wish. A reunion with a family he had lost. A family that could never have been.

"I was always looking for you," he reached up to touch her face, but his arms were too weak so Minnie took his hand and pressed it to her cheek. "You've had a good life?" he asked.

"Very good. I still go to church every Sunday."

"That's my girl," Graypay said with great effort.

"I married a nice man. He was very good to me."

"Was?" Graypay asked.

"He died a while back."

"I'll be seeing him soon," Graypay said. "I'll tell him about you."

Minnie's eyes teared up. "Thank you. And you? You had a good life?"

"I married. Eventually. Had a son. Now a granddaughter. It's been a great journey."

"You must be tired," Minnie smoothed his hair.

Graypay chuckled softly. "I still watch for the fly-bees in the spring."

Minnie laughed. "They will lead you home."

My Last Entry

Graypay

Looking back at the life list I made all those years ago when the world was bigger and people nicer, I see that I really have lived a life of wonders. I traveled. That was my first desire on my list. When I wrote those words: "Travel. Be an explorer" I had dreams of discovering new places, unearthing different paths, making a name for myself as a hero of the west. Such are the dreams of boys. Every place I went was new to me, and therefore undiscovered by my own eyes, my mind, and my soul. That was my discovery.

I have driven myself mad wondering what would have happened if I had just run away with Minnie. In one hand, I held the ever-pressing desire to have kept Minnie with me. In the other, I hold the thankfulness for my life in the west, which brought me so much knowledge and joy, and ultimately Stephie, my son, and then Alison. Would I have those things if I had run away with Minnie? And if I had become her father, although an illegal one, what then?

Guilt for letting Minnie go has driven me down for decades. I'm approaching my last days and have finally become comfortable with the fact that life is a series of events that define us based on our responses to them.

My life, like it or not, does hold many memories that pierce like shards of glass. My life was broken the first time my father hit me, those shards lodging deep in my skin as I headed out west. I did find healing there. Love and family, too. And Minnie. And then the shards returned when her uncle snatched her out of my arms, opening old wounds and slicing a thousand new ones.

I will not leave this earth thinking that my life was one mistake after another. I had excellent years out west and many more with Stephie. Being Alison's grandfather has given much recovery to the deep aches of my soul.

Alzheimer's will be the last shard for me, cutting me away from my body, slicing my mind free from what makes me…me. As my mind shatters, releasing the fragments of my life to the proverbial wind, those little splinters will cut my loved ones. All I can do is offer these journals as a reminder of who I was and what I knew.

Therefore, stay awake! For you do not know on which day your Lord will come. Be sure of this: if the master of the house had known the hour of the night when the thief was coming, he would have stayed awake and not let his house be broken into. So too, you also must be prepared, for at an hour you do not expect, the Son of Man will come.

~ *Matthew 24:42-44*